ABOUT T...

Barbara Cartland, the world'... who is also an historian, play... and television personality, has... sold over 500 million copies all over the world.

She has also had many historical works published and has written four autobiographies as well as the biographies of her mother and that of her brother, Ronald Cartland, who was the first Member of Parliament to be killed in the last war. This book has a preface by Sir Winston Churchill and has just been republished with an introduction by the late Sir Arthur Bryant.

Love at the Helm, a novel written with the help and inspiration of the late Earl Mountbatten of Burma, Great Uncle of His Royal Highness The Prince of Wales, is being sold for the Mountbatten Memorial Trust.

She has broken the world record for the last thirteen years by writing an average of twenty-three books a year. In the Guinness Book of Records she is listed as the world's top-selling author.

Miss Cartland in 1978 sang an Album of Love Songs with the Royal Philharmonic Orchestra.

In private life Barbara Cartland, who is a Dame of Grace of the Order of St. John of Jerusalem, Chairman of the St. John Council in Hertfordshire and Deputy President of the St. John Ambulance Brigade, has fought for better conditions and salaries for Midwives and Nurses.

She championed the cause for the Elderly in 1956 invoking a Government Enquiry into the "Housing Conditions of Old People".

In 1962 she had the Law of England changed so that Local Authorities had to provide camps for their own Gypsies. This has meant that since then thousands of Gypsy children have been able to go to School which they had never been able to do in the past, as their caravans were moved every twenty-four hours by the Police.

There are now fourteen camps in Hertfordshire and Barbara Cartland has her own Romany Gypsy Camp called Barbaraville by the Gypsies.

Her designs "Decorating with Love" are being sold all over the U.S.A. and the National Home Fashions League made her, in 1981, "Woman of Achievement".

Barbara Cartland's book Getting Older, Growing Younger, has been published in Great Britain and the U.S.A. and her fifth Cookery Book, The Romance of Food, is now being used by the House of Commons.

In 1984, she received, at Kennedy Airport, America's Bishop Wright Air Industry Award for her contribution to the development of aviation. In 1931 she and two R.A.F. Officers thought of, and carried, the first aeroplane-towed glider air-mail.

During the War she was Chief Lady Welfare Officer in Bedfordshire looking after 20,000 Service men and women. She thought of having a pool of Wedding Dresses at the War Office so a Service Bride could hire a gown for the day.

She bought 1,000 secondhand gowns without coupons for the A.T.S., the W.A.A.F.s and the W.R.N.S. In 1945 Barbara Cartland received the Certificate of Merit from Eastern Command.

In 1964 Barbara Cartland founded the National Association for Health of which she is the President, as a front for all the Health Stores and for any product made as alternative medicine.

This has now a £500,000,000 turnover a year, with one third going in export.

In January 1988 she received "La Médaille de Vermeil de la Ville de Paris" (the Gold Medal of Paris). This is the highest award to be given by the City of Paris for ACHIEVEMENT – 25 million books sold in France.

In March 1988 Barbara Cartland was asked by the Indian Government to open their Health Resort outside Delhi. This is almost the largest Health Resort in the world.

Barbara Cartland was received with great enthusiasm by her fans, who also fêted her at a Reception in the city and she received the gift of an embossed plate from the Government.

A VERY SPECIAL LOVE

The Marquis of Okehampton has become involved with Lady Yasmin Caton who is beautiful but also, he realises, very dangerous.

A strange Priest calls at his house and informs him that his Ward Zia, whom he has never seen, desires to become a Nun and he has come to ask his permission as her Guardian for her to do so.

The Marquis finds this extraordinary, and even more so when he learns that Zia, the daughter of the late Colonel Langley in whose Regiment he served, has come into a vast fortune.

He tells the Priest he would first like to visit the Convent of the Holy Thorn which is in Cornwall.

When he arrives he is introduced to an extremely ugly and unprepossessing girl whom he is told is Zia.

Extremely intelligent, the Marquis coaxes her into admitting that she is an impostor and is merely attached to the Convent because she has nowhere else to go.

The real Zia manages to escape by climbing over the Convent wall. How, after the Marquis has taken her to London, the false Priest kidnaps her and demands an enormous ransom for her release; and how the Marquis with great brilliance saves her and is instrumental in the Priest losing his life is told in this very unusual and fascinating 424th story by Barbara Cartland.

By the same author in Pan Books

A Hazard of Hearts
The Lady and the Highwayman
A Chieftain Finds Love
A Knight in Paris
Love at First Sight
The Lovely Liar
Paradise in Penang
The Passionate Princess
Revenge is Sweet
Solita and the Spies
Kiss from a Stranger
Real Love or Fake
The Marquis Wins

BARBARA CARTLAND

A VERY SPECIAL LOVE

Pan Original
Pan Books London, Sydney and Auckland

First published 1990 by Pan Books Ltd,
Cavaye Place, London SW10 9PG
9 8 7 6 5 4 3 2 1
© Cartland Promotions 1990
ISBN 0 330 31201 4
Typeset by Selectmove Ltd, London
Printed and bound in Great Britain by
Richard Clay Ltd, Bungay, Suffolk

This book is sold subject to the condition that it shall not, by way of trade or otherwise, be lent, re-sold, hired out, or otherwise circulated without the publisher's prior consent in any form of binding or cover other than that in which it is published and without a similar condition including this condition being imposed on the subsequent purchaser.

Author's Note

Girls are usually accepted into a Convent at the age of eighteen.

A girl first becomes a postulant for nine months, then a novice for two years and it is then, if they still feel they have heard "The Call", they take their final vows at a mystical Religious Ceremony.

Vowing to forsake all others, they become a "Bride of Christ" and are given a gold wedding ring often shaped like a crucifix.

Once they have taken their vows they rarely leave the Order to which they have committed themselves.

But a few who have done so have married, had children, and written a book about their experiences.

Chapter One
1869

The Marquis of Okehampton felt sleepy.

It was not surprising, considering he had for two hours with an insatiable expertise been making love to Yasmin Caton.

She was, he thought, one of the most passionate women he had ever met, besides being one of the loveliest.

At the same time enough was enough and, while he thought it would be an effort to move, he had a sudden longing to be on his way home to his house in Park Lane.

He stirred preparatory to getting out of bed, and Yasmin, who was close against him, said in a low voice:

"I have something to tell you, Rayburn."

The Marquis made a sound which was hardly a question, and she went on:

"I heard this afternoon from Paris that Lionel has collapsed with a very severe stroke."

The Marquis stiffened.

"This afternoon?" he exclaimed. "And you entertained me here at dinner to-night?"

"I told nobody – and I was so looking forward to seeing you."

The Marquis was silent in sheer astonishment.

Lord Caton was an extremely distinguished man who was of great importance to the Queen and had gone to Paris on a special mission to see the Emperor.

He was, although it seemed incredible, forty years older than his wife.

All the more then, if he had suffered from a stroke, as Yasmin had just told him, she should undoubtedly be at his side.

As if she guessed what he was thinking, Lady Caton said:

"Naturally I am leaving for Paris first thing to-morrow morning, but I had to see you, Rayburn, I had to!"

"Then, if you are leaving early . . ." the Marquis began.

He would have moved away from her, but she put her hand on his chest to prevent him from doing so, saying as she did so:

"I have something else to tell you."

"What is it?" he asked.

"I am going to have a baby!"

The Marquis was stunned into silence.

"What we have to do, dearest," Yasmin Caton went on, "is to wait until Lionel dies, which according to the letter I have received will not be long, then be married secretly, perhaps in France."

The Marquis thought he could not be hearing aright, as she continued:

"Then we can go on a long, long honeymoon before we announce that our marriage has taken place several months previously. Although the child will be born prematurely, there will be no question of it not being yours."

The Marquis was still speechless as she moved a little closer to him and said in a caressing voice:

"We will be very happy, dearest, and when I am your wife all my dreams will come true!"

The Marquis was aware that a great number of women had thought that if they could marry him it would be the dream of their lives.

But he had no intention of marrying anybody, least of all a woman with whom he was having an *affaire de coeur*.

There had been a great number of women in his life, which was not surprising, considering he was not only exceedingly handsome and attractive, but also one of the wealthiest men in England.

Ever since he left Oxford he had been pressured towards marriage.

His relatives had almost gone down on their knees to beseech him to settle down and have an heir.

He had been absolutely determined that nobody, definitely nobody, should choose his wife for him.

He was not certain exactly what he wanted, but it was certainly not a woman who in becoming his mistress had been unfaithful to her husband.

His contemporaries in the smart Social World in which he lived would have laughed at him for having such ideas.

It was the Prince of Wales who had made it for the first time easy for a man to have an affair with a woman of his own class.

His Royal Highness's interest in the *Princesse de Sagan* and other beautiful women had naturally caused a great deal of comment.

It had altered the rules of Society which, while unwritten, were invariably obeyed by those who were accepted socially.

The Marquis had therefore made love to the lovely women who attracted him, without his behaviour being considered in any way outrageous.

He had thought Yasmin Caton to be one of the most beautiful creatures he had ever seen.

From the first moment they had been introduced there had been a vibration between them which made it inevitable what the outcome would be.

At least that was what he had thought, but now it appeared from what Yasmin had just said that the tale was by no means at an end.

He was not only astounded by what she had told him, but horrified.

The Marquis had been in many dangerous situations.

But it flashed through his mind that this was more dangerous than anything he had encountered before.

Bullets had missed him by a hair's breadth, and by a miracle his life had been saved at sea.

He knew now another miracle was needed if he was to escape from a trap in which he would be a prisoner for the rest of his life.

The Marquis was astute and very quick-witted, but for the moment he felt as if his head was filled with cotton-wool and he was finding it difficult to know what to say or think.

How could he have imagined for one moment that Yasmin Caton would contrive to force him to marry her?

She had put him in a position where it would be impossible for him to refuse to make what the servants called "an honest woman" of her.

His first thought was that perhaps things were not as bad as she thought, and Lord Caton would not die.

Then he knew, if he was honest, that the last time he had seen His Lordship at Windsor Castle he had thought he looked drawn and tired, and even older than he actually was.

The Marquis strove wildly to find words in which to answer Yasmin, but before he could do so she said:

"I love you, Rayburn, I love you with all my heart, and as I know you love me, what could be more wonderful than that I should give you a son?"

She spoke in a gushing voice which he thought now he had heard her use before on several occasions, and considered it too effusive.

Then, almost as if he was being helped by some power beyond himself, a conversation came back to him.

It had taken place soon after he first met Yasmin Caton.

He remembered sitting in White's Club with one of his special friends with whom he had served in the same Regiment.

His name was Harry Blessington, and they had been discussing the next house-party the Marquis was to give at Oke Castle, his ancestral home in Sussex.

He seldom gave a party without Harry being present, especially when it was one that included the Beauties in whom they were both interested.

Slowly, as if he was feeling his way through dark clouds, the Marquis made himself recall what had been said.

"I suppose you are asking Yasmin Caton?" Harry asked. "I saw you with her last night."

"She is unusually beautiful!" he had answered.

"I agree with you and my mother, who knows her family, has often said it was a crime to make a girl who was so lovely marry a man old enough to be her father."

"I suppose as Caton was rich and important, they considered that was all that mattered," he replied cynically.

"Of course," Harry agreed, "and they rushed Yasmin up to the altar before she was even eighteen and obviously had no idea what a crashing bore Caton could be!"

"I have hardly ever spoken to him."

"I had him next to me for two hours the other night at a dinner at Windsor Castle," Harry groaned, "and he droned on until I thought I should go mad!"

"In which case," he remembered saying with a twist of his lips, "I must obviously console his wife."

"He married again to have an heir," Harry said reflectively, "as his first wife only produced daughters, but my mother told me that once again he has been frustrated."

The Marquis had not been listening to Harry with much attention, but now he was sure Harry had finished by saying:

"The beautiful Yasmin had a fall out hunting a year after they were married, and that apparently put paid to any hopes she might have of producing a son!"

While giving only one ear to Harry's story, the Marquis was thinking how beautiful Yasmin Caton was.

He was also planning how he would have the opportunity of telling her so very much more eloquently than he could do in words.

Now, like a light in the darkness what Harry had told him came flooding back.

He knew now that Yasmin was trying yet another trick, and, God knows, he had encountered quite a number to get him up the aisle.

The numbness that had encompassed him and muddled his brain vanished.

He could think clearly, he was after all not trapped, and his one idea was to get away without a scene.

Aloud he said:

"I think you are looking too far ahead. What you have to do now, Yasmin, is to leave for Paris, and hope that nobody is ever aware that I dined with you after you received the letter telling you of your husband's illness."

"I have locked it away in my jewel-case," Yasmin replied.

The Marquis only hoped her lady's-maid would not have any opportunity of reading it.

Aware how servants gossiped, he knew a story like this would circulate round Mayfair quicker than the North wind.

"You were very sensible," he said, "but now I must leave you."

Yasmin tried to hold onto him, but he rose from the bed and started to dress.

As if she thought it was important for him to realise how beautiful she was, she lay back against the pillows, her body looking, as he had told her earlier, as translucent as a pearl.

As the Marquis adjusted his tie in the mirror over the mantelpiece, he could see her very clearly behind him.

He thought now she was not beautiful but merely dangerous.

He had never been foolish enough to think she was a clever woman, but he had not realised that she was such a determined one.

He could now understand that if she was debarred from enjoying all social activities for a year while she was in mourning for her husband, she would realise she might easily lose him.

She had therefore thought out the only way in which she could make him feel completely and absolutely beholden to her.

If, as she was planning, they were married within a month or two, or perhaps even sooner, there would be no reason for him to learn until some time later that the baby was just a myth of her over-active mind.

The Marquis shrugged himself into his long-tailed evening-coat as he walked to the side of the bed.

Yasmin held out her arms, but he knew if he kissed her she would pull him down on top of her and once again it would be hard to escape.

Instead he took both her hands in his, kissing first one, then the other.

"Take care of yourself, Yasmin," he said in his deep voice.

"You will think of me, dearest, wonderful Rayburn?" she asked. "You know that I will be counting the hours until I see you again."

The Marquis did not answer.

He only moved towards the door, and as he opened it Yasmin cried:

"Wait! I have something else to say . . ."
She was too late.

The door closed before her sentence was half-finished, and she could hear the Marquis moving quickly down the thickly carpeted stairs to the front-door.

Outside his carriage was waiting, and as soon as he appeared the footman jumped down from the box to open the carriage-door.

He was a little earlier than usual and he had been half-afraid they might not yet have arrived.

Unlike many of his contemporaries, he was extremely considerate towards his servants.

If he knew he was not likely to be leaving the house where he had dined much before two o'clock, he would order his carriage accordingly.

It always irritated him to know that his coachman and his horses were waiting outside and resenting the fact that they were kept out so late.

Now as he stepped into his carriage, the footman put a light rug over his knees.

The Marquis thought to himself as he did so that, like a fox, he was running to ground.

There were only a few seconds in which to save himself from being torn to pieces by the hounds.

How could he have imagined that Yasmin Caton would sink so low as to try to deceive him with the oldest trick in the world?

If it had not been for Harry Blessington's mother, he would be in an impossible position.

He would have had to agree to Yasmin's insistence that he should marry her the moment she was free.

A lesser man might have refused to do so, because the child was in the eyes of the Law her husband's.

But that, the Marquis knew, would be at the expense of betraying his every instinct of how a Gentleman should behave.

It was something which would have made him ashamed of himself for being what the members of White's would undoubtedly call a "bounder".

Women could cheat, and no-one thought the worse of them. In fact as one wit had said:

"No Lady has to be a Gentleman!"

But the unwritten laws of being a Gentleman were very strict, and any man who broke them was liable to be thrown out of his Club and ostracised by his friends.

At the same time, when he reached his house in Park Lane the Marquis had to face the fact that he was not entirely "out of the wood".

If Lord Caton died, and it seemed inevitable that he would, Yasmin would surely continue to try to deceive him.

Though he had avoided a scene to-night by not telling her what he suspected to be the truth, there would inevitably be scenes in the future.

The idea of it made him shudder.

If there was one thing the Marquis really disliked it was tears and recriminations from a woman in whom he was no longer interested.

It always meant cries of "Why do you no longer love me?", "What have I done to lose you?", "How can you be so cruel?"

That made him feel as if he would never be able to show any interest in a woman again.

And yet inevitably a few days later he would see another lovely woman and be aware of the invitation in her eyes and a provocative pout on her lips.

Then he would feel once again the first warmth of desire and know that sooner or later she would end up in his arms.

"The trouble with you, Rayburn," Harry had said once, "is that you are too damned good-looking!"

The Marquis had laughed.

"That is hardly my fault!"

"Your father was one of the best-looking men I have ever seen," Harry had gone on, "and your mother was lovely! I can understand he found it difficult to find anybody to take her place although there must have been plenty of applicants."

"That was true," the Marquis thought now.

When his valet had helped him undress and he was in bed, he found himself thinking of his mother rather than Yasmin.

When she died she was still beautiful, even though her hair was white and her face was lined.

As a young girl she had been breathtakingly lovely, but it was not only her beauty that mattered, the Marquis thought, it was because she was so sweet, gentle and loving.

What was more, he was quite certain that the only man who had ever touched her had been his father.

She would no more have thought of being unfaithful to him than of flying to the moon!

"How could I possibly contemplate marrying somebody like Yasmin, beautiful though she is," he asked himself, "and have to wonder how many men sitting at my table have been her lovers, or likely to become so?"

At the same time the girls he had met, and there were not many, seemed gauche, plain and usually painfully shy.

They had of course been paraded in front of him whenever their ambitious Mamas got the chance: at Balls, house-parties where the hostess had an unmarried daughter, and even at dinner-parties.

He would find himself next to a girl of eighteen and know exactly why she was his dinner-partner.

How could he ever marry somebody, however suitable from a worldly point of view, who would bore him stiff from the moment he put a ring on her finger?

His thoughts were once again on Yasmin, and before he went to sleep he made up his mind if possible never to see her again.

He was quite certain he would be bombarded by her with letters, but that was nothing unusual.

If and when Lord Caton died, they were not likely to run into each other at a party because for a year, following the example set by the Queen, she would have to forgo all social activities.

When the Marquis was called at eight o'clock the following morning, he felt as if, after a terrible nightmare the night before, the sun was now shining.

He went down to breakfast in a buoyant mood.

Then almost as if the ghost of Yasmin was haunting him, he had a sudden longing for the country.

He knew that to-day he was supposed to have luncheon with the Prince of Wales.

To-night there was a dinner-party for a Ball at which he would meet his special friends and many of the Beauties who were captivating the Social World at the moment.

He had the feeling that every beautiful woman would look to him like Yasmin, and he would be suspicious that beneath the surface there were lurking lies, deceptions and danger.

"I will go to the country," the Marquis decided.

He rose from the breakfast-table and walked into his Study which was an attractive room overlooking a small garden at the back of the house.

He knew as he did so that the Butler would notify his secretary where he was, and his secretary would bring his letters to him there.

Mr. Barrett was an elderly man who had been with his father during the last years of his life, and his staying on was the chief reason that the Marquis's estates were run so well.

His houses were kept stocked with excellent staff, and his engagements carefully detailed so that none was ever forgotten.

The Marquis had seated himself at his flat-topped Georgian writing-desk when Mr. Barrett came into the room.

"Good-morning, My Lord!" he said respectfully. "I am afraid I have rather more letters to-day than usual."

As he spoke he placed two piles down on the desk, one the Marquis knew were private letters which Mr. Barrett was too discerning to open.

The other and larger pile were invitations and appeals from charities which ran into an astronomical number during the year.

"Is there anything important, Barrett?" the Marquis asked.

"No more than usual, My Lord, except that there is a Priest here who wishes to see you."

"A Priest?" the Marquis asked. "Begging, I suppose! Surely you can deal with him?"

"He has called, My Lord, regarding Miss Zia Langley."

The Marquis stared at him as for a moment he could not place the name.

Then he asked:

"Do you mean Colonel Langley's daughter?"

"Yes, My Lord. You will remember she is Your Lordship's Ward."

"Good Heavens!" the Marquis exclaimed. "I had forgotten all about her! Now I think of it, the girl was being brought up by one of her relatives."

"That is correct, My Lord, I knew I could rely on your memory," Mr. Barrett said admiringly. "When Colonel Langley was killed, his sister-in-law, Lady Langley, had the young lady to live with her and sent her to School."

"And what has happened? Why am I involved?" the Marquis asked.

"I think Your Lordship must have forgotten, although I did tell you six months ago, that Lady Langley had died."

The Marquis could not remember that, but he did not interrupt and Mr. Barrett went on:

"The notice of it was in the newspapers because Lady Langley left her niece her fortune, which was a quite large one."

The Marquis thought that in that case he would not be expected to support his Ward whom he had never seen.

The background of the situation was that Colonel Terence Langley had been his Commanding Officer when he was in the Household Brigade.

He was a charming man and a magnificent rider, and he had befriended the Marquis as soon as he joined the Regiment.

Because they were both absorbedly interested in horses they had spent quite a lot of time together, apart from their Regimental duties.

Colonel Langley had stayed at Oke Castle, and the Marquis had stayed in the Colonel's house in the country when he was arranging a Point-to-Point or a Steeplechase.

There had been one occasion, he remembered, when there had been a particularly dangerous course.

Before they set out the Colonel had said:

"I suggest that all you young men, if you have anything to leave, should make a Will, just in case anything happens to you."

This advice was a tradition and they had all laughed. Some of them had made ridiculous Wills which they read out aloud.

When they had finished somebody had asked the Colonel somewhat impertinently:

"What about you, Sir? Have you not made your Will?"

"Not for a long time," the Colonel admitted.

"Then come on," everybody shouted, "you cannot give orders and not do what is right yourself!"

Good-humouredly and, the Marquis thought later, because they had all had a lot to drink, the Colonel had written a Will in which he distributed his worldly goods.

He had left his house to his wife, his horses to his brother, his Polo ponies to an Officer of the Regiment, and his pigs and cows to various friends.

Only when he had finished, after bequeathing a number of other items, did the Marquis say:

"What about your daughter? We have never been allowed to see her, but I believe you have one."

"I am not having all you young bloods turning her head!" the Colonel answered. "But now you mention it, Rayburn, I will leave her to you! You are the richest of this bunch, and at least when I am not there you can give her a Ball and make her the Belle of the Season."

The others had laughed uproariously at this.

But the Marquis, who had not then come into the title, had replied that if the Colonel should die that day the only ball he would be able to pay for would be a football!

Everybody thought this was very funny, and they were cracking jokes as they mounted their horses for the Steeple-chase, in which fortunately nobody was killed.

It was just three years later that Colonel Langley was involved in a fatal carriage-accident.

After his death it was discovered he had never made a later Will than the one he had made before the Steeple-chase.

His wife was killed with him, and the Marquis, as he was now, found himself the Guardian of the Colonel's daughter.

He had however been abroad when the Colonel and his wife were buried, and Mr. Barrett had duly sent a wreath with the correct message to the Funeral.

He had waited until the Marquis returned before he told him of what had occurred.

"Good God!" the Marquis had exclaimed. "What am I to do with a child on my hands? How old is she, by the way?"

"She is fifteen, My Lord, and there is no need for you to worry about her. In your absence I got in touch with her Aunt, Lady Langley, the Colonel's older sister.

"She is having Miss Zia to live with her, and will arrange for her education."

The Marquis had given a sigh of relief.

"Thank you, Barrett. I might have known I could rely on you!"

"Lady Langley is very well off, My Lord, so although the Colonel was unable to leave his daughter very much money, she will have everything she needs."

The Marquis had never thought about her again.

Now he asked:

"Why has this Priest come to see me?"

"He has brought with him a letter from Miss Zia Langley," Mr. Barrett replied, "and here it is!"

He put the letter as he spoke down in front of the Marquis and because there was something a little odd about the way he spoke, the Marquis remarked:

"I presume you have already read it. What does it say?"

"Miss Langley asks your permission to become a Nun!"

"A Nun?" the Marquis exclaimed.

He picked up the letter as he spoke and read it.

Dear Guardian,
I wish to take the veil in the Convent of the Holy Thorn and I am told I have to ask your permission to do so.

I should be grateful if you would allow this for I know that here I shall be able to devote myself to the worship of God.

I remain,

Yours respectfully,
Zia Langley.

The Marquis read the letter, then he said:

"This seems somewhat extraordinary! How old is the girl now?"

"The Priest says she is just eighteen."

"And you say she has recently inherited a large fortune from her Aunt?"

"Yes, My Lord!"

The Marquis looked down again at the letter. Then he said:

"I think I had better see this Priest."

"I thought that was what Your Lordship would wish," Mr. Barrett said.

"What did you think of him?" the Marquis enquired.

Mr. Barrett hesitated.

"I may be mistaken, but I have a feeling he is not a particularly – Holy man. Of course, Your Lordship may think differently."

"Have you any reason apart from your instinct for thinking that?" the Marquis asked.

"He was here before I was down this morning," Mr. Barrett answered, "and when the servants offered him coffee he asked for a brandy! He explained that he had had a long journey from Cornwall, but it seemed strange for a Priest."

"I agree with you," the Marquis said briefly. "Send him in!"

He knew as he waited that Barrett had a particularly shrewd instinct and seldom made a mistake where the staff in his houses was concerned.

Only a few moments elapsed before the Butler opened the door to say:

"Father Proteus, M'Lord!"

A man came into the room wearing a cassock.

He looked over forty with just a touch of grey at his temples.

He was a fairly large man, well-built, and certainly, the

Marquis thought, he did not look as if he denied himself in any way.

He wore a large decorative crucifix on his breast, and he moved with deliberately slow dignity across the room to where the Marquis was sitting.

The Marquis held out his hand saying:

"Good-morning, Father, I understand you wished to see me."

"God bless you, my son," the Priest said and sat down opposite the desk in the chair the Marquis indicated.

"This is a very great pleasure for me, Your Lordship," he said as he did so. "I have heard about your success on the race-course, and you must have been very gratified at winning so many of the Classics."

"I am indeed!" the Marquis answered. "You are interested in racing?"

"I try in a very limited way to be aware of what goes on in the world outside," the Priest replied, "and of course, Zia Langley has spoken of what a fine horseman her father was."

"He was indeed," the Marquis agreed. "It is sad that he should die when he was a comparatively young man."

"Very sad indeed," the Priest said, "but he is undoubtedly in Heaven, and all he will worry about is that his daughter should be looked after and protected."

"Protected from what?" the Marquis asked bluntly.

"The wiles and wickedness of this sad world," the Priest replied. "Frankly, My Lord, Zia wishes to take the veil, and I can promise you we will look after her and keep her happy until she joins her father in Heaven."

"And you need my approval for this?" the Marquis asked.

It seemed to him there was a slight change of tone in the Priest's voice as he said:

"If your Lordship would just sign these papers, then I will trouble you no further."

As the Priest spoke he put down on the table two papers; one, the Marquis saw, gave his permission as Guardian for Zia Langley to take the veil.

The other paper was a form which instructed a Bank to transfer money they held in her name to the Convent of the Holy Thorn.

The Marquis stared at the second paper. Then he asked: "Is this transference of money necessary?"

"Those who dedicate themselves to God give up their personal possessions," the Priest said.

"I know that this, where Miss Langley is concerned, will be quite a considerable sum!" the Marquis remarked.

"It does not matter to us, when a woman wishes to take the veil, if there is very little or a great deal," the Priest said pompously. "Everything is dedicated to helping the poor and needy, and there are, as Your Lordship knows, a great many of those at this present time."

"'The poor and needy' who will benefit are in Cornwall?" the Marquis asked.

He had a feeling that the Priest was somewhat surprised by the question, but he answered:

"There are some naturally within our jurisdiction, but we also contribute to the work of our brothers and sisters in London, and in other great towns where there is suffering and, in many cases, starvation!"

"I suppose I should have asked this question before," the Marquis said, "but I gather yours is a Roman Catholic Convent, while Colonel Langley was, as I know for a fact, a Protestant!"

"No, My Lord, you are mistaken," the Priest said. "We are a Teaching Convent for pupils who come to us for tuition not only in the Scriptures, but in other subjects as well."

He paused then went on:

"I persuaded Lady Langley to send Zia to us because we have the best teachers in Music and Art, in which she is interested. She came first as a day-girl."

His voiced deepened dramatically as he continued:

"When Her Ladyship went to God, she voluntarily entered the Convent as a boarder, and she has been so happy with us that she has no wish ever to leave us."

"It sounds very interesting," the Marquis said, "and of course it is something I would like to see for myself, and also to make the acquaintance of my Ward."

Watching the Priest closely, the Marquis was sure he stiffened before he said:

"That is quite unnecessary, My Lord, and I would not wish to impose on Your Lordship's good nature by asking you to make such a long journey.

He paused before he continued. "As Zia says in her letter, she is anxious to take the veil immediately, and we shall have a Special Service within a week or so in which she can do so."

He learnt forward to say even more insistently:

"All Your Lordship has to do is to sign these two papers, and I will not trouble you any further."

"It is really no trouble," the Marquis said lightly. "I was intending in any case to leave London, and instead of going to my Castle as I had decided to do, I will come to Cornwall. I see from the address that your Convent is not far from Falmouth."

The Priest was silent, and before he could speak the Marquis went on:

"I will travel in my yacht, and I should be able to call on you the day after to-morrow. Shall we say at twelve o'clock?"

"This is all really quite unnecessary, My Lord!" the Priest protested. "I am sure Your Lordship will find such a long journey irksome just to see a young girl who will be at her prayers."

"Then I will wait until she has finished them!" the Marquis said.

He rose to his feet as he spoke and very reluctantly the Priest rose too.

"I am sure," the Marquis said genially, "you would, Father, like some refreshment before you leave. Perhaps a light meal? It is, I know, difficult to get good food on the trains."

He held out his hand as he spoke.

The Priest hesitated, then reluctantly, almost as if he was forced to do so, he shook the Marquis's hand.

"I wish I could persuade Your Lordship not to waste your time," he said.

"I cannot believe it will be a waste of time," the Marquis said, "and I think you will understand that I would not wish to be remiss in anything that concerns the Colonel's daughter."

There was nothing the Priest could do but move towards the door, and as the Marquis rang the bell the Butler opened it.

"Good-bye, Father! I will see you on Thursday," the Marquis said.

If the Priest murmured anything in reply he did not hear it.

He waited until a few minutes later Mr. Barrett, as if he knew he would be wanted, came back into the room.

"You were quite right, Barrett," the Marquis said, "there is something wrong here."

He held out the two papers the Priest had given him as he spoke. Mr. Barrett read them and said:

"I think, My Lord, I should get in touch with the Head Office of this Bank and make enquiries as to exactly how much is deposited there in Miss Langley's name."

"That is what I expected you to say," the Marquis said, "and I am suspicious, very suspicious, Barrett, about the whole set-up. Find out to whom the Convent of the Holy Thorn is affiliated."

He paused and then continued:

"I doubt if either the Archbishop of Canterbury, or the Cardinal of Westminster Cathedral has any connections with it."

"I will find out everything I can," Mr. Barrett said. "In fact, My Lord, I have already heard somewhat strange stories about this particular place."

"You have?" the Marquis asked. "You did not mention the fact before."

"I did not wish you to be prejudiced before you had seen the Priest," Mr. Barrett said, "and I have really nothing specific to relate except that one of my relations lives in a village not far from the Convent."

"That might be useful," the Marquis said. "What does he say about it?"

"I saw him about a year ago and I happened to mention Colonel Langley, whom he admired as he had sold him several horses for the Regiment."

"Go on!" the Marquis prompted.

"He had met the Colonel's daughter Zia, and he also knew her Aunt, lady Langley, who sent her to the Convent as a day-girl."

"That is what the Priest told me," the Marquis said.

"My relative said he thought it was a strange set-up. There were several Nuns, most of whom had been there a long time, and the School, which was more or less separate from the Convent."

The Marquis was listening intently as Mr. Barrett went on:

"They managed to collect a number of elderly teachers who had settled in that part of Cornwall."

Mr. Barrett paused.

"This of course resulted, My Lord, in quite a number of the County families sending their daughters there for special lessons — Music in particular, and Art for another."

The Marquis nodded.

"The Priest," Mr. Barrett went on, "and there are a number of them who run the place, are not accepted by the local Clergy. It is only hearsay, but a great amount of alcoholic drink passes through the Convent gates."

Mr. Barrett's eyes twinkled as he added:

"There is always, according to my relative, enough money to pay the Farmers for the best young lambs, chickens, eggs and cream, which locally is considered strange fare for those who profess to be fasting a great deal of the time!"

"I get the picture," the Marquis laughed, "and that is why I am going to Cornwall!"

Mr. Barrett looked at him in astonishment.

"You are really going yourself, My Lord?"

"Most certainly! Let the Captain of the *Unicorn* know that I shall be boarding her this afternoon, and I have informed my visitor that I shall be with him the day after to-morrow."

Mr. Barrett laughed.

"You always do the unexpected, My Lord, and your father had the greatest respect for Colonel Langley."

"So had I!" the Marquis answered.

He did not say any more, but began to sort through his letters.

There was a smile on Mr. Barrett's lips as he sat down on a chair next to the desk and opened his pad ready to take notes of the Marquis's instructions.

Chapter Two

The Marquis joined his yacht immediately after luncheon.

Before he left he wrote explanatory letters to the Prince of Wales and to his hostess for that evening, as well as to several other people with whom he had engagements for the next two or three days.

He was not certain exactly what he intended to do after he had visited the Convent, but he was determined not to come in contact in any way with Yasmin.

Nor did he intend, if Lord Caton died, to attend his Funeral.

He knew it was inevitable there would be some comment about his behaviour.

The question was – where should he go?

He was however intent on finding out first about the Convent of the Holy Thorn.

He remembered hearing in the past that women were welcomed in Convents if they had a fortune with which to endow the Community.

At the same time, mostly this happened in the case of Catholics who had been educated in a Convent School since childhood.

Alternatively women who had had an unfortunate love affair which had made them feel that no other man would ever fill the place of the one they had lost would dedicate their life to God.

At least, he told himself as the *Unicorn* sailed out of

Folkestone Harbour, this was something new for him to do and would help him to forget Yasmin.

Because the weather was warm and sunny and the sea comparatively calm, he was glad to be at sea.

He had not been in his yacht for some time, but he always insisted that it should be ready to leave at a moment's notice.

This was in fact a subtle way of keeping his crew on their toes, and now he appreciated the advantage of such an order.

Everything appeared to be spick and span and the Captain was delighted to welcome him aboard.

"We were hoping you were coming to try out the new engine, M'Lord," he said.

"I have not had any opportunity until now," the Marquis replied, "but I wish to be at Falmouth by to-morrow night, or at least by Thursday morning."

"There's no difficulty about that, M'Lord,' the Captain said confidently.

He proceeded to show the Marquis how fast the *Unicorn* could move, and he was on the bridge most of the afternoon.

In a way he regretted that he had not invited Harry along with him.

Then, he thought, he did not want anybody in London to know why he had left so precipitately, and it would make too good a story to say he was visiting a Nun.

He had left a note for Harry, saying he had to visit Colonel Langley's daughter who was his Ward.

"I will not be away for more than two or three days," he wrote, "but she has been left a fortune and I am obliged to sort things out."

He told Harry to continue to arrange the House-Party at Oke Castle which would take place the weekend after next.

He knew Harry would be curious, but there would be plenty of time to tell him the truth if it was necessary after he returned and swear him to secrecy.

As he moved down the coast he was aware that he was escaping from a trap which Yasmin had set for him, but he was not yet entirely free.

If she insisted on claiming that she was expecting his baby and took a number of her friends into her confidence, it would undoubtedly be very uncomfortable, to say the least of it, for him to prove otherwise.

Now he thought it over, he realised as he had never done before that Yasmin had an iron determination when it came to getting her own way.

She had certainly handled him in a subtle manner that had made him think that he was doing the chasing.

When he looked back, however, he realised that it was always Yasmin who arranged their meetings, and planned each time before he left her, when they would next be together.

Because he had been infatuated by her beauty he had been content, knowing that to make love to her was what he wanted himself.

Now he thought, and in fact it was something he had often thought before, that he disliked being the hunted rather than the hunter.

It was extraordinary how women managed to get their claws into him almost before he knew their names.

As he had a very forceful personality, this seemed rather strange.

He was honest enough to admit however that he had a weakness, which contradicted the rest of his character, when it came to beautiful women, who could always twist him round their little finger.

"I am damned if I will ever let that happen again!" he swore.

But he had to admit to himself that women were as essential in his life as were his horses.

When he went to his cabin after an excellent dinner

provided by one of the Chefs he employed at Oke House, he slept peacefully.

He had chosen the furnishings of his yacht with great care, remembering how he had often disliked the discomfort of the beds in other people's yachts and houses.

He had taken care to choose mattresses on which, his friends told him, it was like "floating on a cloud".

Certainly he did not notice the turbulence of the sea which was due to the wind that came with the dawn.

When he awoke a little later, there was only a slight swell that was not in the least disagreeable.

They sighted the coast of Cornwall late in the afternoon, and were actually moving into Falmouth Harbour by dusk.

The Marquis congratulated the Captain, ate an excellent dinner and retired to bed early.

He made his plans and sent Winton the Mate, who was an intelligent man and had been in the Royal Navy, ashore to find a Livery Stable.

The Marquis had instructed him to hire the most up-to-date Chaise that was available, and the very best horses.

By the time he was having breakfast, he was informed that although the Chaise was slightly old-fashioned, it was well-sprung, and the horses were young and comparatively well-bred.

"That is good!" the Marquis approved. "And they tell me, Winton, that you are a good shot."

"I was when I was in the Navy, M'Lord," the Mate replied, "but I've not used a rifle or a pistol for some years."

"I think it is a skill you are not likely to forget," the Marquis said, "and I want you to come with me to-day and carry a pistol with you."

He rose as he spoke from the table in the Saloon and went to a drawer in a piece of furniture that was fitted to the wall of the cabin.

There were three pistols in it and the Marquis took one out and handed it to Winton.

"I will tell you why it may be necessary on our way to where we are going," he said, "and we leave at eleven o'clock."

"Very good, M'Lord."

The Marquis liked the way the man responded to his instructions without asking any questions.

He knew a great deal about all the men he employed on the *Unicorn* and he was aware that Winton was spoken of as being very quick with a rifle.

He had also at one time boasted that with a pistol he could hit a playing-card thrown into the air through the centre of it.

As the Marquis drove away from the Quay he found that the horses were exactly as Winton had described.

He therefore settled down to enjoy his drive to the Convent which Mr. Barrett had told him was about five miles inland from Falmouth.

The countryside was very beautiful.

Although the Marquis had never visited Cornwall before, he could understand why Cornish people extolled their County.

He remembered he had two friends with estates here to which they were volubly devoted.

Then he knew that Winton was waiting to hear what lay ahead, and he said, choosing his words carefully:

"I may be wrong, Winton, but I rather suspect that a fraud is taking place at a Convent to which we are going now.

"While I am inside the building, I want you to use your eyes and see if you think there is anything suspicious going on, and of course to listen attentively to anything anybody says to you."

He looked at the man to see if he was paying attention and went on:

"I also wish to leave quickly, if it is necessary. If by any chance, which is very unlikely, anybody tries to prevent me from doing so, be ready to fire your pistol, not at the person in question, but over his head to frighten him."

"I understand, M'Lord," Winton replied.

The Marquis noted with amusement that there was a note of excitement in his voice that had not been there before.

He knew that like all young men, he was looking forward to what might be a skirmish, or, if not, certainly an adventure.

It was a few minutes before noon when the Marquis, having followed Mr. Barrett's instructions and the sign-posts, saw the walls which he guessed must enclose the house and the grounds of what had once been a private residence.

He knew he was not mistaken as he drew up at two big, wrought-iron gates and saw they were surmounted by a coat-of-arms that he was sure must have belonged to a noble family.

The gate-keeper came from a lodge and opened the gates, and as he did so the Marquis noted that he used a key to unlock them.

He drove in but stopped beside the gate-keeper to ask:

"Am I right in thinking this is the Convent of the Holy Thorn?"

"Tha' be roight, M'Lor'," the man replied with a broad accent. "They tells Oi ye were expected."

"Thank you."

The Marquis drove on and found the house was only a short distance in front of him.

It was an attractive building with a gabled roof, surrounded by a garden which was bright with flowers while the lawns were well tended.

The Marquis brought his horses to a standstill at an imposing front-door which again had the same coat-of-arms in stone on the portico.

He handed his reins to Winton and stepped down from the Chaise as the front-door opened and a man stood there wearing a monk's robe.

He bowed awkwardly and the Marquis thought he was a rather surly-looking individual, with a pugnacious chin and heavy body.

He would have looked more at home in a boxing-ring than in a Chapel.

"I have called to see Father Proteus," the Marquis said, "as I expect you already know."

"Come this way," the man said, walking ahead heavily in shoes that seemed unnecessarily coarse in contrast to his robe.

He showed the Marquis into a large Sitting-Room overlooking the garden.

He was surprised at the damask-covered sofa and chairs, and there were several pictures on the walls which he was aware were valuable.

He only had time however to have a quick look round before the door opened and Father Proteus came hurrying in.

"Welcome, My Lord!" he said affably. "It is delightful to see you! I hope you had a smooth voyage."

"I enjoyed it," the Marquis said, "and I hope you too did not find your journey from London was too arduous."

Father Proteus held up his hands.

"The train is quicker," he said, "although certainly not and never will be as comfortable as a carriage!"

"I agree with you!" the Marquis smiled.

The door opened, and the servant who had admitted him to the Convent came in with a tray on which there was a bottle of wine and two glasses.

He set it down on a table and Father Proteus said:

"I feel sure, My Lord, you are in need of a little refreshment. It is a warm day, and the dust on roads always makes one thirsty."

The Marquis accepted a glass of wine, aware as he did so that it was an expensive vintage which he sometimes bought himself.

He took a few sips, then said:

"As I am sure, Father, you are very busy, I would like to see Zia Langley immediately."

"Yes, yes, of course!" Father Proteus replied. "She will tell Your Lordship how contented she is with us here, in this happy House of God, surrounded by the beauty of nature."

He spoke in a somewhat theatrical manner, to which the Marquis made no reply.

Father Proteus left the room to return almost at once, so that she must have been waiting outside, with a young woman.

She was dressed in black and wore a dark veil over her head which the Marquis knew was that of a Postulant.

She came towards him, her head bowed, and dropped him a curtsy after which she straightened herself to face him.

As he looked at her the Marquis was shocked.

Zia Langley was undoubtedly a very plain young woman; in fact he doubted if he had ever seen or at least noticed such a plain girl before.

She had a thin face, a large nose and the suspicion of what the Doctors called a "harelip".

It struck him that she was almost repulsive.

She did not look young but might have been any age.

Then as he looked into her eyes which were brown, he saw, again to his surprise, that she was afraid.

"It is a pleasure to meet you, Zia!" he said holding out his hand.

"It was – kind of you to – come and – see me," Zia replied in a low voice which again the Marquis was aware had a note of fear in it.

"I was very fond of your father," he said, "and I can only regret that we have not met before."

"I – miss Papa – very – much."

As she spoke the Marquis was thinking of how good-looking the Colonel had been. In fact he was often teased about it in the Regiment by the other men.

They would say that when he was in his uniform and on parade he looked exactly the handsome Cavalry man the public expected.

"When you are there," a Subaltern said once, "the girls cheer as we ride down the Mall, but they do not give us a glance!"

How was it possible, the Marquis wondered, that such a good-looking man should have such a plain daughter?

Then he remembered admiring Mrs. Langley when he had stayed at their house and thinking she was very attractive.

She had blue eyes and fair hair.

Almost as if the words were put into his mouth he asked:

"I have always wanted to know what happened to Joker."

As he asked the question he saw a blank expression come into Zia's face, and instinctively she looked towards the door which had been left ajar when she entered the room.

The Marquis was sure then that, while Father Proteus had not come in with her, he was listening outside.

Almost as if it was a cue for his entry, the Father appeared in the doorway.

"I was wondering, My Lord," he said, "if you would like Zia to show you the Chapel where she prays and where, when you have given your consent, she will take the veil."

"How kind of you," the Marquis replied, "but I have a better idea. I would like to talk to Zia alone, and as it is such a warm day, I think we should go into the garden and enjoy the sunshine."

Father Proteus frowned, and the Marquis knew he wanted to refuse.

There was a French window in the room and he walked towards it.

Without waiting for Father Proteus's permission, he opened it and stepped onto the terrace outside.

As he did so he was almost certain, although he could not have sworn it in a Court of Law, that Father Proteus took hold of Zia's arm, saying as he did so almost beneath his breath:

"Be careful what you say."

There were three steps down onto the green lawn, and when Zia joined him the Marquis walked away from the house towards the flowerbeds bright with flowers.

"This is a charming garden!" he said conversationally but rather louder so that his voice would carry. "I am sure you enjoy being in it."

"Yes – My Lord."

The Marquis walked even further away from the house, at the same time admiring the flowers that were in the shadow of some trees.

He knew that they were being watched by Father Proteus from the window and walked on still further with Zia beside him.

Her head was bent as if she was too shy to look at him.

When he was certain they were completely out of ear-shot and it would also be difficult for Father Proteus to see them unless he moved to another window, the Marquis said:

"Do not be afraid. I promise I will not hurt you in any way."

The girl beside him looked up and now her eyes were wide with what he recognised was fear.

"I want your help," the Marquis said, "and I need it badly! As I am sure you are a good girl, I am pleading with you to tell me the truth."

"I – I do not – understand."

"I think you do," the Marquis said. "Where is Zia? Why is she not allowed to see me?"

The girl drew in her breath and would have looked wildly back at the house if the Marquis had not put his arm round her shoulders in what might have been an affectionate gesture.

"Trust me," he persisted, "and, as I have already asked, help me!"

"How – did you – know I was not – Zia?" the girl whispered.

"Because you are not in the least like her father or mother."

"They – they chose me – because I am – so ugly they thought you would think there was – nothing strange in my – wanting to take – the veil."

"I guessed that," the Marquis said, "but where is Zia?"

"Locked in – her room – until you – have gone."

The Marquis could see a wooden seat just ahead of them under some trees and he led the girl to it and sat down.

As she sat too he took her hand and slipped it through his arm.

"Now look as if we are having a happy, confidential talk about your childhood."

"They will – kill me if – they think I have – betrayed them," the girl said miserably.

"What is your name?" the Marquis asked.

"Sister – Martha."

"And what is your position in the Convent?"

"I am a Nun – as I have been for two years – and I have very little to do – with the pupils who come – here for – tuition."

"But you know why they want to keep Zia?" the Marquis asked.

Sister Martha nodded her head.

"She – is very – rich – and they are – always wanting – more money!"

"Who are 'they'?"

"Father Proteus – and there are – four other men – who run the – Community."

"Are they really Priests?"

"I do not – know – Father Anthony, an old man who was here before they came, is very ill and his sister was – the Mother Superior – who looked after the – Nuns – like myself."

"And what has happened to her now?"

41

"She died and Father Anthony – does not know – what is – going on!"

"What *is* happening here?" the Marquis asked.

"I do not – really know," Sister Martha replied, "but there was – another girl who was – rich like Zia – and she was – forced to become a Nun because they – wanted her – money."

"What happened to her?" the Marquis enquired.

The Sister looked away from him.

"Tell me!"

"I – I am – afraid!"

"They cannot overhear you," the Marquis said.

There was silence, then in a voice he could hardly hear Sister Martha said:

"She – she tried to – escape – and I think they – killed her!"

The Marquis drew in his breath. Then he said:

"You have to help me, Sister, and if you do so I promise, when Zia gets away from here, I will have this whole place investigated."

"They will – kill me," Sister Martha said, "if they – think I have – told you – anything!"

"They will not know you have said anything that has made me suspicious if you will do exactly as I say."

"I – am – afraid!" she murmured. "I know – what is happening – is wrong and – wicked – but I have – nowhere else to go – and nobody wants me because I am so – ugly."

"Listen to me, Martha," the Marquis said in a quiet voice.

She turned her face to look up at him and he said:

"I promise you that if you help me to get Zia away from here, I will see you are provided for for the rest of your life. If you want to go into another Convent, that shall be arranged for you. If you want to be free I will find somewhere for you to live with people with whom you can be happy."

He saw the Sister look at him as if she could not believe what he was saying.

He smiled at her in a way women found irresistible before he went on:

"Just trust me, and help me, as no one else can do."

He felt the Sister's fingers tighten on his arm as she said:

"I – will try – but I – know that Father Proteus is – watching us."

"Then what we have to do," the Marquis said, "is to convince him that I believe you are Zia, and that I am prepared to sign the documents he has prepared for me, which state that I am quite happy to leave Zia Langley here."

He saw that Sister Martha was looking at him in a bewildered fashion and he went on:

"As soon as Zia is released will you tell her that I have come to rescue her."

"But – how?" Sister Martha asked. "How – can you – do that?"

The Marquis thought for a moment.

Then he looked through the trees to where he could see the walls that surrounded the whole Convent.

"Do not turn your head," he said, "just tell me if there is any place where Zia could climb over this wall."

"There is – one place," Martha replied, "at the – end of the garden – there is an oak tree that Zia can climb."

She was speaking very softly, and after a moment she went on:

"Once she – climbed the tree to – look out and – Father Proteus saw her and was – very angry! She was – punished by being – put on bread and water for – three days!"

The Marquis's lips tightened, but he did not say anything.

"Will she be allowed into the garden after I have gone?" he asked after a moment.

"We are allowed to walk on the lawn within sight of the windows twice a day," Sister Martha said.

"And what is the last time you do so?"

43

"At four o'clock before we have our tea, and after that we are locked in for the night."

"Very well," the Marquis said, "at four o'clock tell Zia when she is in the garden to get as near to the tree as possible, then make a sudden dash, climb it and I will be waiting for her on the other side of the wall."

"It will be – difficult," Martha said unhappily.

"If it is, and she is prevented from escaping, tell her I will come to the Convent this evening, and take her away by force!"

Martha could not prevent a little cry from escaping her lips.

"Be careful!" she warned. "The servants Father Proteus employs are very strong, and since Zia is being – forced into – becoming a Nun they patrol the grounds to make certain she – cannot escape."

She saw the Marquis square his chin; those who knew him, as Harry did, would have been aware that he was very angry.

Then he said:

"You are very brave, Sister, and I admire you very much. Now, when we walk back I want you to look happy, as if I have agreed to everything you have asked of me, and when I have said good-bye, I know Father Proteus will be pleased with you."

"Who was – the 'Joker' of whom you – spoke?" Martha enquired.

"He was a magnificent stallion which Zia's father always rode, and won a great number of Steeplechases on him."

"They – did not tell me that."

"If you had been able to answer that question plausibly, I had several others," the Marquis smiled.

He rose to his feet but kept Sister Martha's arm through his.

"We are going back now," he said, "as I do not wish Father Proteus to be in the least suspicious. When I leave they will think I am returning to my yacht, but make quite certain that Zia is aware that I am waiting for her."

"Once you have gone – I am sure they will – release her."

Once he was certain which was the oak tree at the end of the garden Zia must climb, the Marquis walked with Sister Martha slowly back towards the window from which they had left the Sitting-Room.

As they came within ear-shot of Father Proteus he said in a clear voice:

"I remember your father taking a six foot jump and making us all follow him! We would have looked very foolish if we had failed, when an older man had succeeded!"

As he spoke the Sister was looking up at him as if she was thrilled by every word he said.

"Your mother was also a good rider," the Marquis went on as they reached the steps up into the Sitting-Room, "at least, so I have been told, although actually I never saw her on a horse."

He climbed the steps and seeing Father Proteus in front of him exclaimed:

"I have been talking to Zia about the old days. I suppose, Father, that the pupils in the Convent are not allowed to ride?"

"It can be arranged if it is something they are eager to do," Father Proteus replied. "In fact I have often thought that amongst the other subjects in the curriculum, riding should be included."

"It is certainly the best exercise in the world!" the Marquis said. "But then, I am prejudiced."

"Of course," Father Proteus answered. "And Your Lordship has the finest horses."

They went into the Sitting-Room and the Marquis said to Sister Martha:

"Good-bye, dear, it has been delightful meeting you, and I entirely understand why you wish to spend the rest of your life in this lovely place."

He had taken her hand in his and the Sister replied in a breathless voice:

"Thank you, My Lord! Thank you very – very much!"

She curtsied, then as if she was shy she went from the room leaving the Marquis alone with Father Proteus.

"A charming girl," the Marquis said. "It is sad when her father was so handsome that she should be so plain."

"I thought Your Lordship would understand why she would be happier with us than in the outside world," Father Proteus replied.

"Of course," the Marquis agreed, "and it is probably the right solution. At the same time it is a great pity, and in a way unfair, that some women should be so beautiful and others extremely ugly."

"We can only believe," Father Proteus said, "that God knows best, and there are compensations, as for Zia, in finding the beauty of their souls."

The Marquis sighed, then said:

"I must get back to my yacht. I have, as you will understand, a great number of engagements in London."

"I am sure you have, My Lord, and it was very generous of you to spend so much time on poor little Zia."

The Marquis moved towards the door.

"One moment, My Lord," Father Proteus said hastily. "I think you have forgotten that we need your signature on the form of consent for Zia to take the veil."

"So you do!" the Marquis exclaimed. "How stupid of me! I have left the papers in my yacht."

"I am sure I can provide you with duplicates," Father Proteus said.

"There is no need to trouble," the Marquis replied. "I will sign them before I leave Falmouth and give them to the Harbour Master. You will be able to collect them to-morrow."

"Yes, of course, My Lord," Father Proteus agreed, "but it will take only a few minutes for me to find you the duplicates."

The Marquis drew out his gold watch.

"You must forgive me," he said, "but I have somebody waiting for me, and I am late already."

He had reached the front-door almost before Father Proteus realised what was happening.

Shaking the Priest hurriedly by the hand he reached his hired carriage and sprang into the driving-seat.

"Good-bye, Father!" he called, raising his hat.

"God go with you, my son," the Father answered.

His words were lost in the whirl of the Marquis's wheels and the crack of his whip.

He was down the drive and out of the gates which had been left open for him before Father Proteus moved.

With a smile of satisfaction on his face he walked back through the open door.

The Marquis waited until they were some distance away from the Convent before he asked:

"Did you notice anything strange while I was inside, Winton?"

"Nothin' much, M'Lord," Winton replied, "'cept there was several men lookin' out of different windows. Seemed a bit odd in a Convent which I thinks was for women!"

"That was observant of you," the Marquis replied. "Now, what we are going to do, Winton, is to kidnap a young lady who is being held prisoner there, get her to the yacht and out to sea, before the men you saw looking out of the windows can stop us!"

"'Ow are we goin' t'do that, M'Lord?"

"It will not be easy," the Marquis replied. "They may want to make quite certain we have left, so look back and see if by any chance we are being followed."

Winton did as he was told, finding it difficult to peer through a cloud of dust which the horses and the Chaise raised on the dry road.

After straining his eyes for some minutes he said:

"There's no-one in sight, M'Lord."

"Then look out for the first Posting Inn we come to where we can have something to eat," the Marquis said, "and then we will return!"

He could tell that Winton was excited, but he said nothing, only looking ahead of him.

Suddenly Winton said:

"There it be, M'Lord! That's th' main Highway which I notices when we was comin' 'ere. There must be a Inn o' some sort where th' Stage Coaches stops."

"You are quite right, Winton," the Marquis agreed, "and if there is one, we will find it!"

About a quarter-of-an-hour's drive further on they came to an attractive little Inn called *The Cock and Hen*.

It was obvious the Landlord was very impressed by the Marquis and, while he could not offer him an elaborate meal, what was obtainable was edible.

The Marquis was wise enough not to sample the wine, but enjoyed the home-made cider.

When he had finished and no longer felt hungry, he said to the Landlord:

"Tell me about the Convent you have near here."

"A strange place, Zir, to be sure," the Inn-keeper replied. "They do say th' lasses th' Gentry sends there be well taught, but the Priest who runs it be an odd cove!"

"Is he a Cornish man?"

"Not as Oi understand it, Zir, an' they as be wi' 'im are not the sort Oi loiks t'see in t'Bar!"

The Inn-keeper obviously did not wish to say any more, and picking up the bill the Marquis settled it, including a very generous tip.

The Inn-keeper bowed respectfully as he said:

"Thank ye, thank ye! Oi 'opes Oi moight 'ave t'pleasure o' servin' ye again!"

The Marquis thought that was unlikely, but he did not say so.

He went out of the Dining-Room where they were the only guests, to see that the Inn-keeper had retreated behind the Bar.

He asked him if he had a map of the neighbourhood.

"Oi doubts there be one, Zir," he replied, "but Oi can tell ye anythin' ye wishes to know."

"Well, suppose," the Marquis said, "I take the Convent of the Holy Thorn as a centre point which we both know. What I wish to do is to travel behind it as if I was going North, then turn and approach it from that direction rather than the way I have just come."

It took a little time to explain to the Proprietor exactly what he wanted.

He was then told there was a lane which would take him about half-a-mile North of the Convent, so that when he approached it from there he would be facing South.

This was exactly what the Marquis required and, following the Proprietor's directions, he and Winton set off.

By this time it was after three o'clock and they only had a short way to go before they saw the Convent ahead of them.

The Marquis realised there was no entrance apart from the gates in the South wall through which he had passed earlier.

At exactly four o'clock he drew up on the narrow road below the ancient oak which Sister Martha had told him Zia could climb.

He told Winton to change his seat from the one beside him to the one behind which was intended for a groom.

Then looking up at the boughs of the tree he found himself praying that Sister Martha had been able to tell Zia he was waiting, and that she would be able, unless Father Proteus was suspicious, to reach the oak tree.

He listened and he thought, although it might have been his imagination, that he could hear voices in the garden.

Then suddenly there was a rustle amongst the leaves overhead and the next moment he saw the face of a girl peering over the wall.

It was then he said to Winton:

"Quickly! Catch her!"

Putting his pistol down on the seat, Winton jumped down from the Chaise, and went to the wall.

The girl flung her legs over the wall, and holding tightly to the top of it, she lowered her body with a swiftness which told the Marquis she was athletic as her father had been.

Then as she hovered above his head Winton grasped her ankles.

Suddenly there were shouts, then a shrill scream from the garden.

"Quickly!" the Marquis ordered.

A second later Zia sprang into the Chaise beside him and the horses were already moving as Winton jumped up behind.

"They . . . saw me!" she gasped.

"I heard them!" the Marquis said grimly. "Hold tight! The quicker we get away, the better!"

He cracked his whip and the horses surged forward.

There was a long expanse of the wall to pass before they came to the South entrance of the Convent.

Just before they reached it, Father Proteus ran into the centre of the road waving his arms, and behind him were four other men running through the gate.

The Marquis did not slow his speed.

He drove his horses straight at Father Proteus, and only at the last moment when the Priest realised what was intended did he try to move out of the way.

But it was too late.

The wheel caught him, and there was a scream as he fell to the ground, and a bump as it passed over his leg.

As it did so, Winton fired his pistol twice over the heads of the men who were reaching out to grasp at the Chaise as it passed them.

They instinctively ducked and as they did so the Marquis, driving at a great speed, enveloped them in a cloud of dust.

He drove on for some distance before an excited voice beside him said:

"You have . . . saved . . . me! You have . . . saved me! How can . . . you have been . . . so wonderful?"

Chapter Three

The Marquis, intent on his horses, did not turn his head until they had travelled some way.

Then when he realised they were quite a distance from the Convent he looked round at Zia.

He saw two very large, dark blue eyes in an exquisite little face which he thought was outstandingly pretty.

Then he decided that the right word was "lovely".

She was, he thought, exactly what he had expected the Colonel's daughter to be, and he said with a smile:

"Now I know you really are your father's daughter!"

Zia laughed.

"It was very clever of you to guess that Sister Martha was impersonating me."

"Not really," the Marquis answered. "I could not believe that your father, who was one of the most handsome men I have ever met, could have produced anything so plain!"

"You saved me!" Zia said. "I cannot think how to thank you."

"We will talk about that later," the Marquis replied. "For the moment, the quicker we can get away, the better!"

They drove for some way in silence before Zia said:

"Sister Martha told me you promised to look after her, and Father Proteus will certainly punish her. If he throws her out of the Convent, she has nowhere to go!"

"We must rescue her as quickly as possible," the Marquis said, "and you must tell me how you managed to get yourself in such a mess."

There was silence, and since he thought perhaps it was embarrassing he said quickly:

"Keep it until I have you safely in my yacht."

Zia gave a little cry of excitement.

"You came in your yacht?"

"I thought perhaps Father Proteus might have told you that."

"He told me nothing!" Zia said. "When I was locked in my bedroom I guessed something was happening, but there was no way I could escape."

As the road was twisting and narrow at this point the Marquis had to drive carefully in case they should encounter another vehicle coming in the opposite direction.

He did not therefore ask the question to which he was curious to know the answer.

Only when they drove down to the Quay and he saw the *Unicorn* looking very large and white ahead did he think with a sense of relief that they were out of danger.

A seaman was waiting to go to the horses' heads and the Marquis, putting down his reins, alighted, then went round the Chaise to help Zia to the ground.

But without any assistance she sprang out with the swiftness of a young fawn.

Now he could look at her properly, he saw that she was in fact, as he had already ascertained, very beautiful.

At the same time, she looked somewhat strange with her long gold hair flecked with red falling over her shoulders.

She was wearing a hideous black dress made of some coarse material, and when she started to walk towards the gangway he realised she did so in her stockinged feet.

He knew without being told that she had been given a pair of the thick-soled ugly shoes which were worn by Nuns, and she had kicked them off so as to be able more easily to climb the tree.

As the Marquis reached the deck where the Captain was

waiting, he said to him:

"Put to sea, Captain Blackburn, with all possible speed, and make for Plymouth."

"Very good, My Lord."

The Marquis followed Zia into the Saloon and as she heard the engines starting up beneath her she clasped her hands together and cried:

"I cannot believe . . . this is . . . true! I thought I was . . . doomed and the . . . only way I could . . . escape would be by . . . dying!"

The Marquis replied quietly:

"It is all over now, and I think we should celebrate by having a glass of champagne."

"That is . . . what Papa used to do when he . . . won a . . . Steeplechase!" Zia said.

The Marquis gave the order for the champagne, and by the time it arrived the yacht was out of the harbour and into the open sea.

Zia was watching through the porthole and as the ship began to feel the pressure of the waves she said as if she was speaking to herself:

"Now I am . . . no longer . . . afraid!"

"Come and sit down," the Marquis said. "Drink a little of your champagne, and tell me exactly what happened."

Zia obeyed him and he thought that despite the movement of the yacht, she had an unmistakable grace in the way she walked.

"I was a Day-girl at the Convent while my Aunt Mary was alive," she began, "and when she died . . . Father Proteus suggested that I came to stay as a Boarder for a . . . little while . . . until I could find . . . a relative or somebody else to . . . chaperon me."

"Why did you not write to me?" the Marquis asked.

"Had I done so before I went to the Convent you might have received my letter. I wrote several times after I arrived there, until I was aware there was no hope of your ever receiving them."

The Marquis frowned.

"That man who calls himself Father Proteus must have planned it from the moment he heard you were your Aunt's heiress."

"I realised that . . . afterwards," Zia said in a low voice, "and of course . . . after the Funeral, when the Solicitor told me how . . . rich I was . . . everybody was . . . talking about it."

The Marquis was about to comment, but she cried:

"If you only know how I have gone over it, night after night, and thought how I should have got in touch with you, or some other relatives, before I . . . listened to . . . Father Proteus!"

"I quite understand that it seemed the easiest thing to do at the time," the Marquis said.

"I was so upset at losing Aunt Mary, and also Cornwall was a long way from the people I had known when Papa and Mama were alive, but it was . . . stupid of me . . . very stupid."

"Stop blaming yourself," the Marquis replied. "You could hardly have guessed that the man who called himself a Priest was nothing more or less than a criminal."

"When he told me I had to . . . take the veil," Zia went on, "I thought he . . . must have . . . gone mad! Then I was moved into the Nuns' part of the house away from the pupils who came every day for their lessons, many of whom were . . . my friends. It was then I . . . realised I was . . . his prisoner."

"It must have been very frightening!" the Marquis said sympathetically.

"I was . . . terrified!" Zia admitted. "I had no idea that the men Father Proteus employed, who only came in for a few hours every day, were thugs who would knock anyone out, or ill-treat . . . an intruder."

Zia paused then went on:

"If they had caught . . . us just now when they came . . . through the gates . . . they would undoubtedly have knocked you unconscious . . . if they had not . . . killed you!"

"I can hardly believe it!" the Marquis said. "It seems incredible to me that these evil characters have not been discovered before now."

"Sister Martha said she told you about . . . the other heiress whom they . . . undoubtedly killed once they had their . . . hands on her . . . money."

"Did nobody investigate her death, or make any enquiries?" the Marquis asked.

"They said she had fallen down a flight of stairs and . . . broken her neck," Zia replied. "Which in fact was . . . what she had . . . done, except that . . . they had . . . pushed her!"

There was a little tremor in her voice that told the Marquis it was what she had expected might happen to her.

"It is all over now," he said comfortingly.

She did not reply, and after a moment, he asked:

"What are you thinking?"

"It passed through my mind that Father Proteus will not give up . . . so easily," Zia said in a low voice. "Also . . . if you intend to report to . . . anybody what has . . . happened then I . . . am sure he will . . . try to avenge himself in some way or another."

"I think that is highly unlikely," the Marquis said. "What I have to do, Zia, and I know you will understand, is to speak to the Lord Lieutenant of Cornwall and also to the Chief Constable."

Zia did not reply and after a moment he said:

"Apart from anything else, we have to save Sister Martha. I promised I would look after her in the future and find her somewhere to live, if she does not wish to go into another Convent."

"She is a very good person," Zia said, "and I think she would be happiest in a Convent, but not . . . like the one we . . . have just . . . left!"

She shuddered and because the Marquis thought it was a mistake to let her go on worrying he said:

"I imagine the first thing we have to do now is to find you something to wear."

Zia laughed.

"I had forgotten how extraordinary I must look! When they moved me into the Nuns' side of the house, they gave me what I am wearing now and took away all my own clothes."

"I dare say we can find you something in Plymouth," the Marquis said, "which will save you from arriving in London looking like a crow, and after that, Bond Street is at your disposal!"

Zia looked at him, then she asked:

"My . . . my money is . . . safe?"

"No one can touch it without my permission," the Marquis replied, "and I will notify the Bank where you are as soon as we arrive at my house in Park Lane."

Zia smiled before she said:

"Thank you! Thank you . . . for thinking of . . . everything! I can hardly believe that I no longer . . . need feel . . . afraid . . . or expect to be . . . killed once Father Proteus has got . . . possession of . . . everything I . . . own!"

"If we can prove that he definitely killed that other girl who was an heiress," the Marquis said thoughtfully, "or conspired with others as an accessory in murdering her, then he will undoubtedly be hanged!"

He knew by the expression on Zia's face that only then would she feel she was completely free.

He told himself it was inevitable, having suffered so much at the man's hands, that it would upset her for a long time.

But he was sure, once she was in a different environment and was enjoying the Social Season in London as she should be doing at her age, it would soon fade from her mind.

Because he thought it was important, he deliberately talked to her of the old days.

He told her how fond he and all his brother officers had been of her father, and praised his brilliant riding.

"I suppose you ride yourself?" he asked.

"I had horses when I was living with Aunt Mary," Zia replied, "but it was not the same as riding with Papa. He always inspired one to do better."

"That is what I think we all felt when we served under him," the Marquis replied.

It was dark before the yacht reached Plymouth.

The Marquis had written two letters which he arranged for the seamen to deliver immediately.

One was to the Lord Lieutenant of Cornwall and the other to the Chief Constable of the County.

He thought it would assuage any nervousness Zia might feel at being still not a very great distance from Father Proteus.

He therefore ordered Winton and another member of his crew to be on guard all night, both of them armed.

The following morning, as soon as the shops were open, Captain Blackburn went ashore.

His instructions were to buy some clothes for Zia which would at least make her look more conventional than she did at the moment.

She had dined with the Marquis the previous night wearing a silk nightshirt and a robe which he wore in the summer, and was therefore made of a thin material.

Because it was much too long, she had turned up the hem and the cuffs with safety-pins.

There was a sash to tie round her small waist, and it seemed in some strange way quite a becoming garment.

Being a deep sea blue, it echoed the colour of her eyes, which the Marquis thought were different from the blue of any other eyes he had ever seen.

He had never actually dined alone with a young girl before.

He had always imagined, when his relatives kept telling him he must take one for a wife, that she would undoubtedly be not only boring but ignorant of anything in which he himself was interested.

Zia, however, looking very young, talked to him of horses about which she knew a great deal.

She also knew the history of her father's Regiment and that of several others in which the Marquis was interested, and was extremely knowledgeable about them.

She asked him intelligent questions about his estate, and because she had always lived in the country, they could discuss rural problems.

These included persuading the labourers to accept new machinery, an innovation of which they were extremely suspicious.

In fact, by late evening the Marquis thought he might have been dining with Harry, for they would have discussed very much the same subjects.

He sent Zia to bed early, knowing that she was tired not only from the drama and anxiety of what had happened during the day.

He knew from what she said that she had not slept properly for a long time, being so afraid of what might happen to her in the future.

He could hardly believe it possible that Father Proteus would have dared to murder her.

Yet what was to stop him, once he had complete control of her money?

When the Marquis himself finally went to bed he was still thinking over what had happened, and what he had heard.

It was hard to believe he had not stepped into a drama that was taking place in a Play-house.

Or he might have been reading a novel in which everything that happened sprang from the frightful imagination of the author who had written it.

It never struck him when he finally fell asleep that he had not given one thought to Yasmin since the previous evening.

The Marquis had finished his breakfast and was wondering if Zia had eaten hers in her cabin, when she came into the Saloon.

For a moment he just stared at her.

Then he realised that if last night she had seemed attractive in his robe with her hair tied back with a piece of ribbon, now dressed as a lady she was breathtaking!

The best that Plymouth could provide was a very simple summer gown of some thin material.

The skirt was full with a small bustle at the back, while Zia's tiny waist was encircled by a blue sash which almost matched her eyes.

The Captain must also have brought her hair-pins, for she had arranged her hair in a *chignon*.

The Marquis noticed she had a long, swan-like neck, besides an exquisitely curved figure.

She stood for a moment in the doorway of the Saloon and as he rose to his feet he said:

"You look now exactly as your father would have wanted you to!"

Zia laughed delightedly.

"I feel more like myself again, and I have already thrown that hideous Nun's robe out of the porthole!"

The Marquis laughed.

"I hope it sank to the bottom, taking all your worries with it!"

Zia sat down at the table and the Stewards brought in the

dishes which had been kept hot until she appeared.

"I forgot last night," she said as she helped herself, "to thank you for the first delicious meal I have had for months! I so enjoyed talking to you that I forgot my manners!"

The way she spoke, the Marquis thought, was quite different from the way any other woman would have expressed her pleasure in his company.

Whereas last night he had thought as he looked at Zia that she was little more than a child, to-day she was a young woman, one he was aware would appear like a shining light in London Society.

He had already planned while he was dressing that he would ask his grandmother if she would present Zia to the Social World.

The Dowager Marchioness, although she was getting on for seventy, was still very active.

She found the Dower House at Oke Castle boring because she was so often alone.

She therefore made every possible excuse to go to London.

She stayed at the Marquis's house in Park Lane, where she had once been the most important hostess in the Social World.

"Grandmama will enjoy having a débutante to look after," the Marquis thought, "and as Zia is so attractive, it will not be difficult to find her a husband."

It struck him that as she was so rich there would inevitably be a multitude of "Fortune-Hunters" who would pursue her.

He told himself that, as her Guardian, he must be careful to ensure that she was married for herself and not for her money.

Now, looking at her, he was quite certain there would be dozens of men who would fall in love with her almost as soon as they saw her.

61

He knew that if he was to be a conscientious Guardian it would take up a great deal of his time.

He was not sure if he resented that or whether it might provide a new interest.

"Are we going to stay here long?" Zia asked as she put down her knife and fork.

It was a simple question.

But the Marquis was aware that she was still frightened that Father Proteus might appear in some devilish way of his own and get her back into his clutches.

"We will leave the moment I have spoken to the Lord Lieutenant," he replied, "but I am afraid, Zia, you will have to answer a certain number of questions about the Convent."

He thought she was going to refuse, and said quickly:

"I know it is uncomfortable for you, but we must think of Sister Martha, and also make quite certain that these criminals do not get other helpless girls into their clutches, who are not as agile as you are at climbing oak trees!"

He spoke lightly to relieve the tension, and Zia answered:

"Of course I must do that, and perhaps the old Nuns will be able to stay on, even though I am sure Father Proteus has either spent or crooked away every penny that was there before he arrived."

The Marquis learnt next morning that the Convent had at first been for older women who had nowhere to go.

Then it had been more or less appropriated by Father Proteus who realised he was onto a good thing.

His friends had moved in and because the old Priest was too ill to argue with them and the Mother Superior was very frail, they had simply taken possession of the house.

There had been no one with enough standing or determination to prevent them from doing so.

"After that had happened," the Chief Constable said, who had arrived at the same time as the Lord Lieutenant,

"Your Lordship will understand that unless somebody complained, there was no reason for me to interfere with what on the surface appeared to be a Religious Institution."

"I do understand that," the Marquis replied, "but now something has to be done."

"Of course it must!" the Lord Lieutenant agreed.

He was a distinguished Peer whom the Marquis had met at Windsor Castle.

When he learnt what had occurred, he insisted that they should take immediate steps against Father Proteus.

The Chief Constable took a statement from Zia.

Then because the Marquis was in a hurry to get away, both the Lord Lieutenant and the Chief Constable promised that when they had investigated further they would send him a report to London.

"You will understand that I shall be very curious," the Marquis said. "At the same time, I should be grateful if you would try to ensure that my Ward's name is not brought into any public statements."

He looked at the Lord Lieutenant as he spoke who said at once:

"I understand your concern, Okehampton, and I will do all I can to prevent anything appearing in the newspapers."

The Marquis thanked him, and as soon as the two gentlemen left told the Captain to put to sea.

"The whole problem is now out of our hands," he said to Zia, "and we can therefore relax and enjoy ourselves."

"It was kind of you to be so concerned about Sister Martha."

The Marquis had said that if Sister Martha was in any distress the Chief Constable was to arrange for her to travel to London and she could stay at Oke House until her future was settled.

"I will of course pay all expenses," the Marquis added, "and also the expenses of somebody to travel with her so that she will not be alone."

Now he said to Zia:

"We must always remember that if Sister Martha had not been brave enough to allay Father Proteus's suspicions, you would not be here now."

"I will give her anything she wants," Zia said positively. "She is really *my* responsibility, not yours!"

"We will not quarrel over her," the Marquis smiled, "and I think we will both see that Sister Martha is very much happier in the future than she has been in the past."

"If only we could change her face, poor thing!" Zia said. "She always talks of herself as being ugly, and I know it worries her."

"I expect, unless she is to go on being a Nun, pretty gowns and her hair arranged in a more attractive fashion would make all the difference," the Marquis remarked.

"We could certainly try," Zia answered, "and it will be like having a handicapped child to look after!"

They both laughed at the idea.

Then to speak of a child made the Marquis remember Yasmin, and her assertion that he had given her a baby.

Once again the anger he had felt at being deceived and threatened swept over him.

As it did so Zia exclaimed:

"W-what have I . . . said wrong? What has . . . upset you?"

She sounded so worried that the Marquis replied quickly:

"It has nothing to do with you—just something I remembered that made me angry."

Then as still she looked at him with worried eyes he asked:

"How can you be aware of what I am thinking? I have often congratulated myself on being perceptive, but it is not something I expected to find in you."

"I think it is something I have . . . always had," Zia answered, "in fact I could often read Papa's thoughts before he had put them into words. Mama said it was because we have Celtish blood in our veins."

"As your Guardian," the Marquis said with mock seriousness, "I forbid you to read my thoughts! They are often not suitable for a well-bred young lady to know about!"

Zia laughed.

"Now you are making me curious and I shall try harder than ever to know exactly what you are thinking."

"Am I to believe that you are defying me?" the Marquis enquired. "In which case, I shall take a very strict line in seeing that you obey my orders!"

Zia laughed again.

"If I am too young to be perceptive, you are certainly too young to be a Guardian! They are usually old with grey hair and in the same category as grandfathers!"

"That is how you should think of me!" the Marquis said.

She gave him a mischievous smile which he thought was particularly attractive before she replied:

"Now you are trying to frighten me, and as I refuse, now I am free, to be frightened any more, you will have to think of a better way to keep me in order!"

He found that as the day progressed Zia seemed for the first time carefree.

She teased him, and had what he could only describe as a *joie de vivre* which made them both laugh a great deal.

The hours seemed to pass more quickly than he could have imagined possible.

He had decided they would stay the night in a quiet harbour, and reach Folkestone early the following morning, when they would take the train to London.

Then he realised he was enjoying himself more than he had thought possible and had no desire to go back to London too quickly.

He therefore told his Captain to sail on round the coast and move up the Thames as he had often done before, to disembark at Westminster.

"I am glad that is what you have decided to do," Zia said when he told her. "I love being at sea, and it is so delightful to be with you because you make me think of Papa."

The Marquis thought with a twist of his lips that when he was with most women he did not in any way remind them of their fathers.

Despite the fact that Zia was laughing with him as if he was a contemporary, he was aware that she did not think of him, as any other woman would have done, as an attractive man.

He supposed it was because she was so young and, as he had already found, completely innocent of the world.

The strange thing was that while there were none of the *double entendres* which were so much part of the conversations he had with the Beauties he and Harry pursued, he found her interesting.

When he thought about it, he had to admit that he had not been bored for one moment since they had been together.

He knew that when Yasmin or any of his previous loves had been alone with him in the yacht, every word they spoke was flirtatious.

Every look of their eyes would hold an invitation.

It would have been impossible for him to be with them for any length of time without holding them in his arms, kissing them, and eventually taking them below to his cabin.

But it obviously had never entered Zia's mind that she should try to attract him as a woman.

When they went to their separate cabins before dinner, the Marquis was changed first and was waiting in the Saloon for Zia to appear.

The yacht was anchored in a small bay where there was shelter from the wind as well as any movement of the sea.

The stewards had not yet turned on the lights in the Saloon, but there were candles on the table which made the dinner laid for two seem very romantic.

The Marquis always looked particularly magnificent in evening clothes, and as he waited for Zia he looked out through the porthole knowing the stars would soon begin to twinkle overhead.

It was a warm evening and he thought any other woman who was with him would be waiting for the moment when they would go out on deck.

She would look up at him, and her long neck and profile silhouetted against the darkness would be alluring and very seductive.

Every movement would be an invitation for him to put his arms around her. Then his lips would hold her captive and he would kiss her until they were both breathless.

He then became aware of the sound of light footsteps coming up the companionway and a second later Zia was in the Saloon.

"Look at me in my finery!" she exclaimed.

She spread out her arms sideways as she spoke and twirled round so that the Marquis could see the movement of her full skirt and the little cascading frill running round the hem.

Her shoulders were bare, and her waist looked even smaller than it had during the daytime.

Her gown was of a very pale green, the colour of buds in the Spring.

With the candlelight picking out the red in her hair, she looked, the Marquis thought, like a Sprite who must have come from the waves.

There was something ethereal about her, and at the same time it was almost as if she moved to music.

"I must certainly congratulate the Captain!" the Marquis said. "His taste is impeccable!"

"That is what I thought," Zia agreed, "and I must now show him how smart I look."

She did not wait for the Marquis to reply, but went out of the Saloon and onto the deck. Then he heard her running forward towards the bridge.

He could not help smiling as he followed her.

He was thinking that none of the Beauties whom he and Harry found so alluring would think the Captain's opinion of their appearance of any importance.

On the other hand they would undoubtedly expect a eulogy from him.

"I must not spoil her," the Marquis told himself as he reached the bridge.

"I'm glad you're pleased, Miss Langley," he heard the Captain say. "In fact my wife always asks my advice before she buys a new gown."

"Then you can tell her that His Lordship thinks your taste is impeccable," Zia answered, "and I think really you ought to come and advise me when I reach Bond Street!"

The Captain laughed.

"I'm a better judge of ships than I am of gowns, Miss Langley, and this is one of the finest ships I've ever handled."

"Now I am receiving the compliments!" the Marquis said as he joined them.

"And quite rightly," Zia said. "The *Unicorn* is magnificent!"

As they moved back towards the Saloon, the Marquis could not help wondering whether she thought the owner of it was magnificent too.

He was so used to compliments from any woman in whom he was interested that he now found, although he admitted it was ridiculous, that he missed them when they were not there.

When they sat down to dinner, Zia found the food as excellent as it had been the night before and quickly forgot about her appearance as once again they were talking of the old days.

"Perhaps I shall not be . . . with you," she said a little wistfully, "but if I am . . . and you have a Steeplechase . . . would you allow me to ride in it?"

"Certainly not!" the Marquis said. "Steeplechases are not for women, but if I arrange a Point-to-Point, which I usually do sometime in the Summer, then I will introduce a 'Ladies' Race' in which you can compete."

Zia regarded him for a moment quizzically before she said:

"As Papa's daughter, if you will lend me one of Your Lordship's magnificent horses, I would much rather race you!"

"And you really think you might win?" the Marquis asked.

He expected her to say that was impossible, but she would like to try.

Instead after a moment she replied:

"I think I might have a sporting chance if you allowed me to choose the horse I want to ride, and then to get to know it before the race."

The Marquis raised his eyebrows and she explained:

"Papa said that while horses love racing, it is always right to explain to them what is happening, and also if they are used to their rider, they know what he expects of them, and will want to please him."

The Marquis wanted to say that she was just being imaginative.

Then he remembered how the Colonel had said much the same thing to his young Subalterns before they rode in the Regimental races in which the Household Brigade always distinguished themselves.

"What I am saying," Zia went on, "is that if I can talk to my horse and let him know that he is to beat yours, perhaps we shall pass the winning-post ahead of you."

"I think you are using magic," the Marquis said, "and that is distinctly a contravention of all the rules of the game!"

Zia merely laughed.

"If I get the chance to show you what I mean," she said, "you will understand."

The Marquis, as it happened, did understand.

He had never before met a woman who knew the secrets which were used by the gypsies and by the jockeys who were most successful in the races in which they rode.

When it was time to go to bed, he admitted that he had enjoyed himself and was also more certain than ever that Zia would be a great success in London.

"She is original, she is unusual and very lovely!" he said to himself.

He decided he would tell his grandmother he would give a Ball for her at Oke House in London, and another at the Castle.

"No girl could ask for more," he told himself, "and, by the time she is dressed better than any other débutante, she will quickly capture some distinguished young aristocrat, and I shall have done my duty nobly as her father and mother would expect me to do."

Then as he tried to think who amongst the young men would be the most suitable as Zia's husband, he found himself discarding first one then another.

They might be "blue-blooded", they might have distinguished names and important titles to inherit.

But when he thought them over, they did not seem to qualify for anybody as unusual or so lovely as Zia.

He knew that with her large fortune, she could certainly pick and choose.

But it was unthinkable to imagine her married for instance to a certain young Peer of his acquaintance who did nothing but pursue actresses and "Cyprians" as he had done ever since he left School.

Two other young noblemen were, to the Marquis's certain knowledge, keeping Pretty Horse-Breakers in smart Villas in St. John's Wood.

From the conversations he had had with Zia, he knew she had no knowledge of what were called "Other Interests" in a man's life.

And she would undoubtedly be extremely shocked when she learned about them.

There was something very pure and innocent in her blue eyes.

As the same time they held a certain mystery which the Marquis was aware was something spiritual and not what was usually associated with the word where it concerned a woman.

"Damn it all!" he said to himself. "There must be some decent man about; a man who would be faithful to a wife if she was like Zia!"

Then he found himself wondering if in the future she would become like Yasmin and all the other Beauties who had given him their favours.

He knew that when he had dined in another man's house in his absence, eaten his food and drunk his wine, then enjoyed himself with his wife, he had always felt slightly ashamed.

To him it was almost like picking someone's pocket.

Yet it was part of the Social World in which he moved.

He more or less accepted that if a husband did not look after his wife or had "Other Interests", there was no reason why she should remain faithful to him.

And yet, he told himself, it was what he would expect of his own wife.

Then, he thought cynically, he was asking too much.

How could he be sure if he was away from home for even one night that his wife would not have a lover creeping up his stairs and into his bed?

Because he felt almost tormented by the idea of it, he threw off the bedclothes and went to one of the portholes in his cabin.

He pulled back the curtains and saw the stars filling the great arc of the sky, their light reflected in the sea below them.

It was very beautiful, and very romantic.

The Marquis looked out for a long time, then he went back to bed saying violently beneath his breath:

"All women are unfaithful, treacherous, and deceitful! I will never marry!"

Chapter Four

The *Unicorn* eventually reached London and drew alongside the Embankment above London Bridge.

Thanks to the Marquis's efficient arrangements, his carriage drawn by two horses was waiting for them and he took Zia ashore.

She thanked the Captain very prettily for the voyage, saying how much she had enjoyed herself.

When they drove off she said with a lilt in her voice:

"This is very . . . very . . . exciting!"

"I hope you will enjoy yourself in London," the Marquis said, "and I also want to show you my Castle in Sussex."

She smiled at him as she added:

"And of course I am longing to see your horses!"

The Marquis was wondering if he could include her in the party he was giving next weekend.

As Yasmin would not be present, there would be an empty place, but he knew it was not the type of party to which he should take a débutante.

"I will leave her in London with my Grandmother," he decided, "and she can come to the Castle the week after."

When they arrived at Oak House in Park Lane he knew that Zia was impressed by the magnificence of the mansion and when she entered, by the furniture and pictures.

He was, as it happened, exceedingly proud of the house itself which had been redecorated by his mother who he always considered had excellent taste.

There was none of the clutter of aspidistras, antimacassars, and the knick-knacks which had become fashionable since Queen Victoria had come to the throne.

The Dowager Marchioness had been brought up in a Regency House.

She admired that period more than any other, thinking it more suitable to her husband than the fashions which had recently come into vogue.

Zia was not aware that she was seeing what the Victorians thought was old-fashioned.

She only knew that it was beautiful and appealed to her in a way that was difficult to express.

The Dowager Marchioness had been informed of her grandson's imminent arrival, and was waiting for them in the Drawing-Room which extended over the whole of the First Floor.

It was a classically beautiful room, hung with pictures that were mostly French, and lit by huge chandeliers with a hundred tapers in each.

It looked to Zia like a Fairy Palace.

The Marquis noted and was surprised that Zia was not in the least shy at meeting his grandmother, who overawed most people.

She curtsied to the Dowager gracefully, then said eagerly:

"I have been longing to meet you, Ma'am, after all His Lordship has told me about your parties which were the most distinguished ever given in London."

The Dowager Marchioness laughed.

"Is that what you expect me to give for you?"

"Oh, no!" Zia answered. "But I was thinking as I came into the room how lovely you must have looked against a background which is almost a scene from a Shakespearean Play."

The Dowager Marchioness laughed again.

"I think, Rayburn," she said to her grandson, "Zia is thinking of us as idealistic figures instead of real and often very tiresome people."

"I am sure that does not apply to you, Grandmama!" he said. "At the moment, I am delighted to be taken as an idealistic figure, rather than a disillusioned human."

He saw his grandmother give him an enquiring glance, and he was aware he had spoken bitterly without thinking.

He therefore quickly told her of how he had rescued Zia from Father Proteus and added when she had listened to him in astonishment:

"It is a story you must keep to yourself, for as you well know, Grandmama, it could very easily be the talk of every Drawing-Room and every Club in London!"

"I have never heard of anything so disgraceful!" the Dowager Marchioness said. "You poor child! You must have gone through agonies before my grandson rescued you!"

"It was very . . . very frightening," Zia agreed, "but His Lordship has told me to forget it . . . and that is what I am . . . trying to . . . do."

"You will forget it as soon as we have bought you the prettiest gowns we can find, and my grandson has sent out invitations for your Ball."

She looked at the Marquis with a questioning look in her eyes and he responded:

"I intend to give one here, Grandmama, and also one at the Castle. It is what I know Zia's father and mother would want me to do."

"Of course they would!" the Dowager Marchioness approved. "And because you want Zia to be asked to everybody else's Balls, you must send the invitations as quickly as possible!"

"I am dreaming this is happening!" Zia said. "It is so exciting that I want to dance and sing, and make quite sure that I do not wake up!"

The Marquis and his grandmother laughed.

Then when they went down to luncheon, the Marquis

could feel her enthusiasm infecting him and thought perhaps it might be quite amusing to give a Ball at Oke House, which he had never done before.

After luncheon the Dowager Marchioness ordered a carriage and said she was taking Zia shopping.

"We will choose from gowns that are immediately obtainable," she said, "and have them sent here for you to try on. We will also order a great number to be made as quickly as possible, and buy the accessories to go with them."

"It sounds a phenomenal task," the Marquis observed. "I am glad you do not want me to accompany you."

"I can imagine nothing we want less!" his grandmother replied. "Like all Englishmen you would sit looking bored and thinking that to be inside on such a sunny day was a crime against nature!"

Zia laughed.

"Of course he would! Papa always said he enjoyed seeing Mama looking beautiful in a new gown, but he had no wish to hear about it before she was actually inside it!"

The Marquis accompanied them to the front-door to see them off in the carriage.

Then he went into his Study where he knew Mr. Barrett had a pile of letters waiting for him.

He was not mistaken, and as Mr. Barrett joined him he said:

"There are two letters, My Lord, which I thought you would wish to see first. One from the Bank giving you a detailed account of Miss Langley's fortune, and the other from the Lord Lieutenant of Cornwall."

"I was hoping I would hear from him!" the Marquis exclaimed.

Mr. Barrett handed him the letter and as the Marquis read it, his expression changed.

"You have read this, Barrett?" he asked.

"Yes, My Lord."

"How could that damned man have got away so quickly? How could he have been aware that the Chief Constable intended to arrest him?"

"Bad news travels on the wind, My Lord," Mr. Barrett remarked.

"I can only suppose what happened was that he learned that the *Unicorn* had docked at Plymouth Harbour, and drew the conclusion that I was communicating with the Lord Lieutenant and the Chief Constable."

'I am sure it must have been something like that," Mr. Barrett agreed, "and as you see, the Lord Lieutenant says there is no one left in the Convent except the Nuns and the old Priest who is too ill to know what is going on."

The Marquis glanced down at the letter again.

"He says he has arranged for Sister Martha to leave for London to-day, so we shall know more when she arrives this evening."

"As it will be very late, My Lord," Mr. Barrett said, "would it not be best for the young woman to go straight to bed and let you have a talk with her in the morning?"

"I will do that," the Marquis said. "At the same time, it worries me, Barrett, that that criminal gang are still at large."

"Does Your Lordship think," Mr. Barrett asked hesitatingly, "that Miss Langley is in any danger from them?"

"One never knows," the Marquis said. "Naturally they will be extremely resentful that she escaped and we are aware of their appalling plan to seize her fortune."

Mr. Barrett looked worried.

Then the Marquis, as if he was reassuring himself, said:

"It would be a great mistake to upset Miss Zia by alarming her, and actually I cannot believe that this man Proteus, which I suspect is not his real name, would be so stupid as to attract attention to himself when he knows the Police are already looking for him."

77

"I am sure you are right, My Lord," Mr. Barrett agreed, "and anyway, now Miss Zia is under the chaperonage of Her Ladyship she will not be going anywhere alone."

"No, of course not," the Marquis agreed.

At the same time, he thought he would make it clear to his grandmother that Zia was not to go to any place where Proteus might be lurking.

He would certainly see when they went to the country that the footman on the box of the carriage always had a loaded pistol in the pocket specially designed for it.

It was something that had been very necessary in the days when Highwaymen were to be found in many parts of the country, especially in the South.

It was some years now since the Marquis had heard of an incident of that sort, and he was sure most people left their pistols at home, or, if they were in the carriage, they were not loaded.

At the same time he assured himself that he was being needlessly apprehensive in thinking that Proteus would risk his freedom, if not his life, in doing anything so outrageous.

Aloud he said:

"I will have a word with Miss Zia, and we certainly do not want the servants talking about it, or the coachmen looking out for trouble."

"No, of course not, My Lord," Mr. Barrett agreed.

He then handed the Marquis the letter from the Bank.

It consisted of several pages of figures detailing deposits and shares.

When the Marquis looked at the last page on which the total had been calculated he was astonished.

He had gathered from what Mr. Barrett had said that Lady Langley had left a large fortune, but it was in fact very much bigger than he had anticipated.

Mr. Barrett was aware of his surprise, and before the Marquis said anything he explained:

"When Her Ladyship married the Colonel's brother, she was not, I gather, very rich, but over the years a number of her relatives died and bequeathed to her a great deal of what they owned. Apart from that, her money has been so well invested that it was in some instances increased a hundred-fold."

"I understand," the Marquis said. "At the same time, it is not always a good thing for a young girl to own so much."

"I am sure Your Lordship is thinking of the 'Fortune-Hunters'," Mr. Barrett remarked.

"I am!" the Marquis agreed. "I look to you, Barrett, to keep a strict watch on the young men who knock on the door, send flowers and *billets-doux*, so that we can 'nip them in the bud', so to speak."

"I think you will find," Mr. Barrett said, "there is hardly a man in London who would not be eager to get his hands on such an enormous fortune, apart from the fact that Miss Langley is one of the loveliest young ladies I have ever seen!"

"I cannot think why I always get myself in this sort of mess!" the Marquis remarked irritably. "You know as well as I do, Barrett, that if she marries the wrong type of man, I shall have it on my conscience for the rest of my life."

Mr. Barrett was obviously thinking of an appropriate reply when the door opened and Harry Blessington came into the Study.

"Hello, Rayburn!" he said to the Marquis. "Thank goodness you are back! I have missed you."

"I am back," the Marquis replied, "and I have a job for you."

"A job?" Harry queried.

The Marquis handed him the letter he had received from the Bank.

As he did so Mr. Barrett slipped away, knowing that the two close friends would have a great deal to say to each other.

Harry read the letter the Marquis handed to him, then gave a long, low whistle.

"I thought you would be surprised!" the Marquis said.

"Surprised? I am astounded!" Harry answered. "Who could have guessed that the Colonel's daughter would turn out to be 'Miss Croesus'?"

"It is a pity the Colonel himself could not have enjoyed some of it," the Marquis commented. "He would have had even better horses than he had already!"

"Tell me what she is like?" Harry asked. "If she is not a good rider, I will never believe in heredity again."

"I have a great deal to tell you," the Marquis said.

As he spoke he sat down in a comfortable chair, and when Harry sat beside him he told him exactly what had happened when he arrived in Cornwall.

Harry listened without speaking until he had finished, then he said:

"Good God, Rayburn! If I did not know you so well I would think you had been drinking! It is all the Theatricals I have ever watched at the Play-house rolled into one!"

"That is what I thought myself," the Marquis said. "The question is – what are we going to do about it?"

"You mean the story is not finished?"

"Not while that fake Priest and his cohorts are still at large! And that is where you have to help me."

Harry looked at the Marquis. Then he said:

"Of course I will. This will give you something new to think about, which, I feel, is rather important at the moment."

"What do you mean by that?" the Marquis enquired.

"I have some bad news for you," Harry said.

The Marquis stiffened.

He knew perceptively before Harry said any more what the news would be.

"I have just heard," Harry began, "that Lord Caton died last night!"

It was what the Marquis had feared but expected to hear.

At the same time, he knew from the tone of Harry's voice there was more to it than that.

He waited, and Harry went on:

"You will not like this, but my friend Irene, who is coming to the Castle this weekend, received a letter from Yasmin Caton yesterday."

The Marquis waited, knowing before Harry spoke what was in the letter.

"Yasmin told Irene, of course in complete confidence," he said, "that you had asked her to marry you as soon as she was free, and that she was carrying your child!"

It was what the Marquis knew he would be told, and yet to hear it spoken out loud hit him like a blow.

He rose to his feet to stand with his back to Harry looking down at the fireplace which, because it was Summer, was filled with flowers.

"It is a lie!" he said heavily after some minutes of silence.

"I know that!" Harry replied. "But what are you going to do about it?"

The Marquis turned round.

"What the devil can I do?" he asked.

Coming back from Bond Street, Zia thought it had been very exciting to see the latest and most elaborate fashions.

The Marchioness had chosen a large number of gowns to be delivered to Oke House for her to try on.

After being forced to wear the hideous black gown she had thrown into the sea and beneath it the coarse cotton underclothes which were correct for a Nun, she had revelled in the silk nightgowns and negligées in the shop that specialised in such intimacies.

"It is all so thrilling!" she said as they drove back to Park Lane. "And how can I thank you, Ma'am, for being so kind to me?"

"I am enjoying myself as much as you are!" the Dowager Marchioness replied. "I suppose every woman dreams of the moment when she can buy the most expensive and the most beautiful clothes available, having a large Bank Account to pay for them!"

Zia was still for a moment, then she said:

"You must help me, Ma'am, to spend a lot of my money on other people who are in need of it."

The Marchioness looked at her tenderly before she answered:

"Of course I will help you, Dear."

"I am sure His Lordship will also be able to advise me," Zia went on, "because I have no wish to find anything I give for those who are starving or ill-treated has been put into the pocket of somebody like Father Proteus."

The Dowager smiled.

"You are very sensible, child, and that is what you need to be. Money is always a responsibility, and I am glad to think you want to help others not so fortunate as yourself."

"Of course I do," Zia replied, "and I would like, if His Lordship will allow me, to send somebody who is competent and kindly to look after the old Nuns at the Convent."

She sighed before she continued:

"They often went short of food while I am sure Father Proteus was stuffing himself in another part of the house!"

"We will talk to my grandson about it," the Dowager Marchioness promised.

"I am only hoping," Zia said reflectively, "that Father Proteus and those horrible men who were with him are now behind bars."

It was a question she asked the Marquis after dinner when his grandmother had gone upstairs to bed, and Harry, who had dined with them, was out of the room.

They had talked about everything else at dinner except Zia's experiences in Cornwall.

Yet she was intelligent enough to realise that the Marquis was keeping something from her.

Now when he came back into the Drawing-Room, having seen his grandmother up the stairs, she said:

"I know you must have heard from the Lord Lieutenant and the Chief Constable. What have they done with Father Proteus?"

The Marquis wanted to lie to her, but thought it would be a mistake.

As he hesitated Zia said quickly:

"He has got away, has he not?"

"Yes," the Marquis admitted reluctantly. "When the police reached the Convent there was no sign of him or his men."

Zia clasped her hands together and he saw the fear was back in her eyes.

"H-he will . . . never forgive me . . . and perhaps whether he has my money or not . . . he will want to . . . kill me."

"Nonsense!" the Marquis said sharply. "You are not to think such things! He ran away because he was frightened, and somebody must have warned him that the police were coming to arrest him."

He spoke very positively as he went on:

"For all we know he may have taken a ship to America, or is hiding in Scotland, or the North of England. He knows there is nothing now he can get out of you."

"But . . . he might take his . . . revenge."

"Not if it is not going to pay him to get it," the Marquis said. "Be sensible, Zia, and remember that now you are with me he knows he has nothing to gain by pursuing you when there are a great many other women in the world from whom he will be able to extort money."

"You . . . are right . . . of course you . . . are right!" Zia said. "At the same time . . . I am . . . frightened."

She shuddered and added in a small voice:

"I have lived under the same . . . roof with him . . . I know . . . how ruthless he was . . . how utterly he . . . concentrates on . . . getting his . . . own way."

"I can only repeat," the Marquis said, "that he will be no danger to you or to me, so let us forget him!"

He saw the worried expression was still on Zia's face and he said:

"Sister Martha is arriving late this evening, and I suggest you concentrate on deciding how to make sure that she is very much happier in the future than she has been in the past."

"She is coming here?" Zia asked. "I am so glad! Father Proteus has not injured her in any way?"

"Perhaps he is not as dangerous as you think he is," the Marquis said.

But he knew by the expression in Zia's blue eyes that she was frightened and nothing he could say would drive away her fears.

It was after midnight when Sister Martha was brought by a Courier chosen for her by the police to Oke House.

On the Marquis's instructions, Mr. Barrett took her upstairs to the Housekeeper who showed her into a comfortable bed-room.

While a maid unpacked the small suitcase she had brought with her, a meal was brought up on a tray.

Sister Martha enjoyed every mouthful of it and afterwards got into bed to sleep peacefully.

When she awoke, which was early because she was used to saying her prayers in the Chapel, she looked round the bed-room which seemed to her very grand.

She was thinking how the old Priest had been too ill to give the Benediction in recent months, when the door opened and Zia peeped round it.

When she saw that Sister Martha was awake she gave a little exclamation of joy and went to her bedside.

"You are here, and it is lovely to see you!" she said.

Then as she looked at her more closely she asked:

"What has happened? How have you bruised your face?"

"Saul hit me!" Sister Martha answered. "You remember him – the man with the scar?"

Zia sat down on the bed.

"I always thought he was horrible, and I was afraid one of them might do something like that. Are you all right?"

"He knocked me down and I think I was unconscious," Sister Martha replied. "When later I was able to enquire what had happened, I found that Father Proteus, whose leg was injured, had left the Convent with all the four men, taking with him everything that was valuable."

Zia looked at her wide-eyed as Sister Martha went on in a shocked voice:

"You will hardly believe it, Zia, but Father Proteus took all the things from the altar; the candle-sticks, the Communion vessels, and even the cross because it was made of silver."

"He is the most evil man who ever existed!" Zia exclaimed. "But why did the police not catch him?"

"They arrived too late," Sister Martha answered. "I heard somebody say that a man had ridden in very late the night you left, and what he told Father Proteus made him know he must escape while he had the chance."

Zia thought this was what the Marquis thought would have happened, that a spy in Father Proteus's employ had watched as the *Unicorn* put into Plymouth.

They would have known then that the Marquis was communicating with the Lord Lieutenant and the police.

"Have you any idea where they have gone?" Zia asked Sister Martha.

She shook her head.

"He might be anywhere," she said, "but I imagine it will be in London."

"Why London?" Zia asked curiously.

"I heard him say once a long time ago when he did not know I was listening: 'I am fed up with this place! It gives me the creeps! I want to be back amongst the bright lights of London!'"

Zia was frightened.

"I must tell the Marquis that," she said, "and, Sister Martha, you have to be very careful of yourself. I am sure he would be furious to know . . . you were . . . here."

"He will not worry about me, or you," Sister Martha said, "now that he cannot get hold of your money."

"He will certainly not be able to do that now that the Marquis is looking after it."

"If you ask me," Sister Martha said, "he will find some other place he can take over, just as he took over the Convent, and where he can persuade people in a thousand other different ways to lend him money."

Zia knew this was true.

Father Proteus had been able to deceive her Aunt into thinking he was a good and helpful Priest.

And there had been a number of other parents in the County who sent their children to the Convent because Father Proteus had promised they would be well educated.

When she thought about it, she knew he had been astute enough to employ a really accomplished Music Master, and a Painter who certainly achieved good results from his pupils.

There were also three elderly and competent Governesses who made a number of other subjects interesting so that the pupils were eager to learn what they were taught.

Later, when she discussed it with the Marquis, she said:

"When you think of it, My Lord, it was an extremely clever way of doing really nothing except to find out what other people wanted. He had a house to live in, and the fees were very expensive, although I now suspect that he did not pay the teachers very generously."

"And nobody had any idea he was anything other than what he appeared to be?" the Marquis asked.

"No, of course not! He talked as if he was a genuine and dedicated Priest, and after Father Anthony was taken ill he occasionally, if there were visitors to the Convent, conducted a Service in the Chapel. But now I know it was sheer blasphemy, for which he ought to be struck down by a thunderbolt!"

The Marquis smiled.

"Let us hope that will happen," he said, "but as we shall never know the truth, let us forget him!"

Zia thought that would be impossible, but she did not say so.

They talked about Sister Martha and the Marquis, with a kindness Zia thought was unusual in such an important man, questioned the Sister as to what she would like to do.

"If you wish to go into another Convent," he said, "I will arrange with the Archbishop of Westminster Cathedral that you are accepted into the best one he can recommend."

Sister Martha drew in her breath, but she did not speak, and the Marquis went on:

"There is another idea which you might find interesting. Why not put aside your Nun's attire for a while and stay, either here or in the country, and find out if you prefer an ordinary life to one of dedication?"

He knew before he said so that Sister Martha would feel embarrassed at the thought of living with them, and he went on:

"I have a feeling you would like to help other people. Now I have a School on my estate in Sussex where the Mistress who has taught in it for many years is growing old."

He saw Sister Martha's eyes light up and continued:

"Mr. Barrett tells me she is already looking for a successor. Until she finds one, perhaps to help her is something you might contemplate doing. She has room in her small house for any assistant I send her."

Before Sister Martha could reply, Zia exclaimed:

"That is a wonderful idea! And if I come to the Castle, as His Lordship has said I am to do, I will be able to visit you and make sure you are really happy!"

Sister Martha was unable to answer because her eyes had filled with tears, and it was impossible for her to speak.

Zia jumped up and put her arms round the older girl saying:

"There is no hurry for you to make up your mind. Just think it over. We will talk about it and then tell His Lordship in a day or two."

"You are . . . very kind," Sister Martha stammered, "and I do not know . . . what to say."

Then because Zia was sure that the Marquis would find tears tiresome, she took Sister Martha out of the Study where they had been talking.

The Marquis was left alone, and he walked to the window to look out into the garden.

He was thinking that few women of his acquaintance would be so kind as Zia was being to the plain little Nun with whom really she had nothing in common.

He could never remember any of the Beauties with whom he had spent his time worrying over anyone except themselves.

He had often thought that they were quite unnecessarily sharp and intolerant even to their personal servants.

"Zia has been well taught by her father," he told himself.

Then he knew it was not teaching that made Zia care for others, but her warm heart, and that was a very different thing.

Now he was alone he was forced once again to remember what Harry had told him, and to know that Yasmin was making sure in a very subtle manner that it would be impossible for him to escape her.

Of course Irene would talk, however confidential the secret might be with which she had been entrusted.

The Marquis knew he was fortunate that where Harry was concerned it would go no further.

Harry had assured him that he had made Irene swear on everything she held Holy that she would not repeat what Yasmin had written to her to another living soul.

But few women were trustworthy.

No one could be sure that Irene would not, of course in confidence, tell another friend, who would tell another, and yet another.

Within a few days the story would be all over London.

"What shall I do?" the Marquis asked himself a dozen times. "What *can* I do?"

As he spoke the words beneath his breath the door opened and Harry came in.

"I am sorry I am late, Rayburn," he said, "but one of my horses has gone lame, and I went to the Mews to see to him."

"You can always borrow one of mine," the Marquis offered.

"That is what I was just going to ask you," Harry replied. "What are you going to do?"

"I was just thinking of going riding," the Marquis replied. "Then we have a luncheon party to-day, to which, if you remember, you are invited."

"Of course I remember!" Harry said. "If there is one person I enjoy talking to it is your grandmother."

The Marquis stared out of the window, as Harry went on:

"By the way, I have not had a chance to tell you how much I admire your Ward. She is lovely, Rayburn, quite, quite lovely! I only hope you enjoy her looks while you have her with you, because she will not be with you for long!"

"For God's sake," the Marquis replied irritably, "do not start harping on about the girl being married, before she has even attended her first Ball."

"I would not mind betting that by her second she will have had half-a-dozen proposals!" Harry said.

The Marquis did not reply, and after a moment his friend said:

"Do stop, Rayburn, looking like a 'bear with a sore head'! If it is Yasmin that is worrying you, I think I have a solution."

"You have?" the Marquis enquired.

He thought as he spoke that Harry was just being facetious.

Because he had lain awake most of the night worrying as to what he should do, he did not find it a laughing matter.

"It is quite simple," Harry said, "and I cannot think why we did not think of it before."

"Think of what?" the Marquis enquired.

"That you should get married!"

Chapter Five

The Marquis stared at Harry, and was about to reply when the door opened and the Butler announced:

"Lord Charles Fane, My Lord!"

A good-looking young man came into the room saying as he did so:

"I have just learnt, Rayburn, from your grandmother that you are back, and decided to come and see you right away."

The Marquis held out his hand.

"How are you, Charles? Behaving badly as usual, I suppose?"

"Of course," Lord Charles replied, "but I wanted to talk to you about your party, as unfortunately Evelyn's husband has returned from the North and therefore she cannot come."

"Another casualty!" Harry exclaimed before the Marquis could speak.

"Hello, Harry!" Lord Charles said. "Who is the first one?"

Realising he had made a mistake, Harry said hastily:

"Rayburn will tell you our troubles."

"Before I do that," the Marquis said, having no intention of confiding in Lord Charles, "would you like something to drink?"

"Naturally!" Lord Charles replied. "I always think your champagne is medically speaking the best tonic I know."

The Marquis laughed and went to the grog-tray, while Lord Charles seated himself in a comfortable chair near Harry.

"I was wondering what had happened to you," he said to the Marquis who had his back to him, "when I happened to see your grandmother, who was accompanied by the most beautiful creature I could possibly imagine!"

"That is exactly what I have been saying," Harry enthused.

"She really is unbelievably lovely," Lord Charles went on, "and if you do not ask me to dinner I shall sit on your doorstep until I can see her again!"

He was speaking lightly, but the Marquis suddenly felt annoyed.

He knew that Charles Fane was one of the most amusing men in London.

At the same time, he did little but trek from *Boudoir* to *Boudoir*, and his love-affairs were too numerous to count.

He was the last man he would think of as suitable to be with anyone as innocent as Zia.

"Now listen to me, Charles," he said as he handed him a glass of champagne, "Zia is young and unspoilt. Harry and I are going to find her a suitable husband among the young men who do not have a reputation like yours. So – keep away!"

Lord Charles stared at him.

"Are you really giving me orders, Rayburn?" he asked. "I have never heard anything so outrageous, and I have no intention of being told to 'Keep off the grass' where anything so delectable and unusual is concerned."

The Marquis felt his temper rising.

Then he told himself that if Zia looked on him as a Father-figure, she would presumably feel the same about Lord Charles, who was two years older than he was.

At the same time, he would take care that she saw as little of him as possible.

92

"Now, what I want to know," Lord Charles was saying, "is where you found her, and who she is."

As the Marquis did not reply immediately, Harry obliged by saying:

"She is Colonel Langley's daughter – you must remember him!"

"Of course I remember him!" Lord Charles replied. "The best rider I have ever seen, and an exceedingly good-looking man! I suppose it is to be expected that his daughter would look as if she had stepped down from Heaven, or wherever angels come from!"

The Marquis walked to his desk.

"If you two are going to continue rambling on in this idiotic way," he said forcefully, "you had better go into another room, although actually I have a lot to discuss with Harry."

Lord Charles finished his glass of champagne.

"I do not know what I have done to offend you, Rayburn," he said, "but I know when I am not wanted! However, I would like to know what is happening about your party?"

"I have decided to postpone it until a later date!" the Marquis replied.

Harry looked at him in surprise, and Lord Charles said:

"Well, that suits me if Evelyn cannot come. I am not really interested in anybody else, unless of course the exquisite Miss Langley will take her place!"

He was being provocative, but somehow the Marquis could not laugh as he ought to have done.

"I will let you know when I am holding another party," he said coldly, "but it will not be for some time."

"I have a feeling you are keeping something from me," Lord Charles complained. "And if you have a party without me, Rayburn, I swear I will be an unremitting enemy! I might even call you out!"

The Marquis this time laughed, but it was not a particularly humorous sound.

"The last occasion we settled an argument that way," he said, "you had your arm in a sling for three weeks."

"Well, I will think of something else," Lord Charles said, "and I promise you it will be very unpleasant!"

The Marquis was suddenly aware that Harry was frowning at him and he remembered that Lord Charles, although they were quite fond of him, was an irrepressible gossip.

He knew therefore it would be a mistake to quarrel with him at this moment.

"Do not be a fool, Charles," he said. "You know if I have a party it would not be the same if you were not there to make everybody laugh. "It is just that with a débutante on my hands, I do not feel that the sort of party Harry and I were planning would be very appropriate, and I can hardly go to the Castle and leave her alone here with my grandmother."

Charles, who was a very good-humoured person, smiled.

"Of course not," he said, "and if you ask me nicely I will stand back and let some of the unfledged chinless young fools say their piece, but I warn you – I will not cut out altogether!"

"I am hoping to find a responsible husband for Zia," the Marquis said heavily, "and you know as well as I do that, like me, you have no intention of marrying."

"You will have to marry sometime, old man, in order to have an heir," Lord Charles replied. "As for me, you are well aware that my brother has three sons, so there is no chance of my coming into the Dukedom."

"It is a great pity," Harry smiled. "You would be the most flirtatious Duke that has ever been known, but undoubtedly the scandals you would create would have you barred from Windsor Castle!"

"I should certainly be grateful for that!" Lord Charles said. "I am so sorry for all those over-dressed Gentlemen-in-Waiting who have to mop the Queen's tears and listen to her eulogising hour after hour on the virtues of the late lamented Prince Consort!"

Harry and the Marquis both laughed.

At the same time, they were thinking how indiscreet Lord Charles was. The Marquis prayed that he would never know about Yasmin, or the unfortunate situation Zia had been in when he rescued her.

Because Harry was so close to the Marquis, he was aware of what he was thinking and changed the conversation by inviting Lord Charles to relate the latest scandals that were being circulated in Mayfair.

As there were quite a number of them, they were still listening and laughing when the door of the Study was thrown open and Zia came running in.

At that moment the Marquis was standing with his back to the fireplace, while Harry and Lord Charles were sitting deep in the leather arm-chairs.

She therefore saw only the Marquis and ran across the room to him saying:

"Look! I must show Your Lordship my new gown! I have never owned anything so beautiful before, and there are dozens coming later for me to try on!"

She drew in her breath and went on:

"And what do you think? I have been asked to a Ball tonight – my first Ball – and your grandmother has accepted for us all to dine with the Duchess of Bedford!"

"Then you must certainly promise me the first dance," Lord Charles said from behind her.

He knew he was behaving provocatively, and he looked at the Marquis mischievously as he rose to his feet.

"Oh, I am sorry!" Zia said. "I did not know there was anybody else here!"

"Let me introduce Lord Charles Fane," the Marquis said, "but I order you to disbelieve every word he speaks!"

"Now that," Lord Charles exclaimed, "is breaking all the Queensberry Rules! I can assure you, Miss Langley, I am in fact a very truthful man when I say you are the most beautiful person I have ever seen!"

For a moment Zia looked surprised.

"Thank you, My Lord," she said demurely, "but I always obey my Guardian."

They all laughed at this, then she said:

"I must now go and have tea with Her Ladyship, but I did want you to see my gown!"

"You look very nice in it," the Marquis said.

She smiled at him, then ran from the room as Lord Charles ejaculated:

"Nice? I ask you! A more inadequate word I have never heard! Surely, Rayburn, you have some poetry in your soul?"

"I have already told you not to spoil Zia," the Marquis replied, "and I too am now going to have tea with my grandmother and warn my Ward once again against listening to you!"

"The fact that she is in your house gives you an unfair advantage!" Lord Charles complained.

But the Marquis was already leaving the room and walking down the corridor.

He had actually reached the hall when he realised that Lord Charles and Harry were behind him.

He therefore stopped just in case Lord Charles took it into his head to follow him up into the Drawing-Room where he knew Zia would be with his grandmother.

Lord Charles was however taking his top-hat, his gloves and his cane from the footmen, and as the Butler opened the front-door he said:

"Good-bye, Rayburn, I shall see you to-night, and I will certainly claim that first dance!"

He walked out through the door without waiting for an answer, and the Marquis looked at Harry.

"He is hopeless," he said, "but what can we do about him?"

"Nothing," Harry answered, "and I am sure Zia has enough sense not to believe everything he will say to her."

The Marquis however was still frowning as he started to climb the stairs.

"We have to make certain she does not have her head turned by flibbertigibbets like Charles, but meets the right sort of man to make her a good husband."

There was silence as they walked up a few more stairs.

Then Harry said:

"I should have thought the answer to that was quite obvious and would certainly solve your problem!"

"What are you saying?" the Marquis asked.

"If you want me to put it into plain English," Harry replied, "the sooner you marry the girl yourself, the better!"

Zia thought the Ball-Room of the Duchess of Bedford's house was the most beautiful scene she had ever imagined.

The ladies in their full skirted gowns with jewels on their heads and around their necks looked like the Fairy creatures who had stepped out from a Picture-Book.

The gentlemen resplendent in knee-breeches and silk stockings, their long-tailed coats blazing with decorations, were also very impressive.

Because it was so exciting, and at the same time so beautiful, she had no idea that she herself was attracting a great deal of interest and attention.

It was impossible for the Marquis, as he was so handsome, to go anywhere without being noticed.

When he entered the Ball-Room with Zia at his side there was a little gasp that seemed to go up from the dowagers sitting together who were watching the dancers.

The gentlemen standing at the end of the room deciding who should be their next partner drew in their breath when they looked at Zia.

She was wearing a gown which fortunately had required little alteration, but even so had only arrived about fifteen minutes before she had to put it on.

It was white, as was expected of a débutante, but ornamented with flowers which were studded with diamanté.

They encircled her décolletage and decorated not only her bustle but also the hem of her skirt so that she glittered with every movement she made.

The Dowager Marchioness had lent her a number of diamond stars which had been arranged in her hair by a skilful hairdresser.

Every man who looked at her thought there were stars in her eyes as dazzling as those which shone amongst her shining curls.

Before they left for the Ball, when she came downstairs, the Marquis had admitted to himself that she was lovelier than any girl he had ever seen.

She was also, he thought, different in every way from what he expected in somebody so young.

At the same time, he told himself, Harry's idea that he should marry her was absurd, and something he had no intention of doing.

While he was dressing for dinner he had thought that Harry's suggestion of marriage was in fact quite clever.

Of course the only way he could really scotch the rumours that Yasmin was spreading about him would be to let the world know he was to be married.

If he announced his engagement it would be quite fruitless after that for Yasmin to continue with her lie about carrying his child.

It was doubtful in the circumstances if anyone would believe her.

Even if they did, the woman was always blamed if she was foolish enough to get into trouble without first ensuring that the man concerned would do the honourable thing and marry her.

The whole Social World was expecting him sooner or later to choose a wife.

Someone who would be a commendable Marchioness to entertain for him in the same brilliant way that his mother and grandmother had entertained the *Beau Monde*.

It was incredible that Yasmin should try so desperately to blackmail him into marriage.

Yet the Marquis was intelligent enough to realise that she could make things very uncomfortable for him if he had no direct answer to her accusations.

Harry realised shrewdly that the only unassailable answer was his marriage to somebody else.

Although the Marquis had made it a rule never to dance if he could help it, he danced with Zia as soon as they reached the Ball-Room.

He saw Lord Charles moving across the room to take possession of her and it was something he was determined to prevent.

"This is very exciting!" Zia said as they moved slowly to the music of a romantic Waltz.

She did not understand but she felt a little thrill run through her breast because the Marquis was so close and holding her.

"I thought it was something you would enjoy," the Marquis replied. "At the same time, you will understand that you must not dance more than once with the same man, and as soon as each dance is over, you return to my grandmother and sit beside her."

"I can see through the window there are fairy-lights in the garden," Zia said.

Without his intending it, the Marquis's hand tightened for a moment on her small waist.

"No! No! No!" he said firmly. "You will not go into the garden with anybody – do you understand?"

"Of course I understand what you are telling me," Zia replied, "but there is no need to sound so ferocious about it!"

She smiled up at him as she spoke and the Marquis felt he had somehow over-reacted to the situation.

"I do not want you to gain a bad reputation at your very first Ball!" he said.

"Your grandmother has told me how I am to behave," Zia said, "and I promised her I would be very good."

"I hope you will keep your promise."

"It might be . . . difficult if one of my . . . partners is very . . . persuasive!"

For a moment the Marquis glared at her, then he realised she was teasing him.

"For goodness sake, Zia, do be sensible!" he begged. "You must be aware that as you are new to London and also my Ward, people will be watching and talking about you."

"Will they?" Zia asked in surprise. "How thrilling! Was it not lucky that your Grandmother and I found this beautiful gown!"

She lowered her voice as she said:

"Your grandmother said I was not to tell anybody, but actually it was commissioned as a bridal gown for a Spanish Princess, and now the seamstresses will have to sit up all night in order to create another in time for her wedding!"

"I expect they will be well paid for doing so!" the Marquis said cynically.

He realised as he spoke that Zia was not listening to him.

She was glancing round the room, then said in a whisper which only he could hear:

"You are . . . quite right! We are being . . . watched! I think it is not only my gown but because . . . you are dancing with . . . someone as . . . unimportant as me!"

"Who has been talking to you?" the Marquis enquired.

Zia laughed.

"Your grandmother, the Housekeeper, all the maids who look after me, and Captain Blessington!"

"What has Harry been saying?" the Marquis asked sharply.

"I shall not tell you because I am sure it would make you conceited," Zia answered, "but I do . . . realise I am very . . . very . . . privileged to be your Ward."

There was nothing the Marquis could say to this, and when the dance was over, he took Zia back to his grandmother.

He had intended to go to the Card-Room, but somehow he found it impossible not to stay in the Ball-Room to see what Zia was doing.

That she was a wild success was indisputable.

He noticed that every bachelor in the room was attempting to fill in her Dance-Card, but there were more partners than dances.

What surprised him was that unlike other débutantes, and there were a number of them present, Zia was talking and laughing with her partners.

Apparently their compliments did not make her feel shy.

Driving home in the carriage with the Marquis and his grandmother she said:

"Thank you . . . thank you for the most . . . exciting evening I have . . . ever spent!"

"You were certainly a great success, my dear!" the Dowager Marchioness answered. "I am quite sure tomorrow there will be a great pile of invitations to similar Balls and to many other entertainments."

"How . . . could this . . . happen to me?" Zia asked in a low voice. "I was so . . . miserable until His Lordship rescued . . . me that I kept wondering . . . how I could . . . d-die."

"You promised me not to think about it," the Marquis

said.

"How can I help it . . . when I seem to have stepped into a new . . . world which is . . . like Heaven?"

"That is what I hope you will go on thinking," the Dowager Marchioness said.

"Do you know," Zia exclaimed as if she had just remembered, "three gentlemen, and I cannot even remember their names, asked if they could call and see me to-morrow, and said they particularly wanted to talk to me alone!"

The Dowager Marchioness glanced across the carriage at her grandson.

In the light of the candle-lantern she saw he was scowling.

"If any of them propose marriage to you," he said sharply, "you are not to accept them without asking me first!"

"Propose marriage?" Zia enquired in astonishment. "Why should they do that?"

"You have to remember," the Marquis said in a hard voice, "you have an unusually large fortune!"

There was silence, then Zia said in a very small voice:

"I never . . . thought of that. Is that the reason why . . . so many men wanted to . . . dance with me?"

"No, no, of course not!" the Dowager Marchioness said quickly. "You were without exception the most beautiful and best-dressed girl in the room, and they wanted to dance with you for yourself. What my grandson is telling you is that marriage is a very different thing to simply finding you suit each other on the dance-floor."

"Of course it is," Zia said, "but I cannot believe . . . any man would want to . . . marry a girl he had . . . seen only once."

Again the Dowager Marchioness glanced at the Marquis.

"I think you will have so much shopping to do that you will not have time to see any of these impetuous gentlemen," he said slowly, "and I will tell the servants to turn them away."

Zia gave a little cry.

"Oh, no, please let me hear a proposal! I have often wondered what a man would say, and if he really does go down on his knees as they do in novels!"

The Dowager Marchioness laughed.

"You are not to be too strict a Guardian, Rayburn," she said. "I remember my first proposal was from an elderly Colonel who was a friend of my father's, and he was so emotional over it that his moustache wobbled, and I wanted to laugh!"

The Marquis said nothing and the Dowager Marchioness added:

"Zia has to learn to handle her own affairs, and when she says 'No', she must make the gentlemen, however ardent they are, believe that is what she means."

As she spoke the carriage drew up outside Oke House, and the Marquis as he was sitting on the small seat was obliged to alight first.

As he walked into the house he was frowning.

Sister Martha heard somebody opening her bedroom door and as she turned from the window saw to her surprise that it was Zia.

"Are you awake already?" she exclaimed. "When I was told how late you came in last night I thought you would sleep until luncheon!"

"That is what the Dowager Marchioness expected," Zia replied, "but I am too excited to sleep, and I wanted to tell you all about the Ball."

"And I'm longing to hear about it," Sister Martha said, "but first I have a confession to make to you."

Zia looked at her curiously.

"A confession?"

"I was thinking about it last night, and praying just now that I can be brave enough to tell you the truth."

"What is it?" Zia asked. "What is wrong?"

"I have – lied to – you," Sister Martha said, and her tone was piteous.

"I . . . do not understand," Zia said.

"I can't go on pretending! I am – not a – Nun, and I only pretended I was one when – Father Proteus came to – the Convent."

"Is that all?" Zia asked. "Well, I think it was a very sensible thing to do."

"Do you – really? You're not – shocked?"

"No, of course I am not!"

"I was afraid when he appeared and said he was taking over the Convent, that if I was not a Nun he might send me away like the poor old women."

"It is the sort of thing he would do!" Zia said.

"I had nowhere to go, and Father Anthony said I could stay there but I was not to take the veil as I told him I wanted to do, until I was twenty-one."

"So you thought Father Proteus would not interfere if he believed you to be a Nun."

"It was a lie – and I'm so ashamed of it," Martha said. "Father Anthony was too ill for me to explain to him what Father Proteus was doing, so I just put on the wimple and the veil of one of the Nuns who was always in bed."

She gave a little sob which was very pathetic.

"After that, everybody called me 'Sister Martha', and sometimes I forgot myself that I was just – plain Martha whom – nobody wanted."

"You are not to say that again!" Zia protested. "I want you, and now it makes it very much easier for you to do what the Marquis suggested, and teach at the School on his estate."

"When he – hears I have lied – he may not want – me," Martha said nervously.

"I do not think he really understands about Nuns and whether they have taken the veil or not," Zia replied. "I suppose if you were a proper Nun it might be difficult, but as it is, you have just, like me, to forget about Father Proteus and start a new life."

Martha wiped away the tears that threatened to run down her cheeks as she said:

"Oh, Zia, you are so kind to me and, if I could start all over again somewhere quite different, and – very wonderful!"

"That is exactly what you are going to do," Zia said.

She thought for a moment before she went on:

"I have a marvellous idea!"

"What is it?"

"It is only nine o'clock, and the Dowager Marchioness is not being called until eleven. His Lordship has gone riding – I asked my maid where he was when I was getting dressed."

Martha was looking at her while she spoke almost to herself, then she said:

"What we are going to do now is to go shopping! I am going to fit you out in the clothes you will wear as yourself, and you can throw away that hideous garment, just as I threw away the one I had to wear."

Martha gave a little gasp and Zia said:

"Take it off! Take it off quickly! I will give you something to wear and I will order the carriage."

She ran from the room as she spoke, and came back a few minutes later with a gown the Captain had bought for her at Falmouth.

It was too long for Martha, but they hitched it up with a belt.

Then Zia arranged Martha's hair which she thought could look attractive if it was washed and curled.

She then placed on top of her head a hat which had also been bought for her at Falmouth.

Picking up the one she had brought to wear herself and which matched her gown, she ran down the stairs with Martha.

The carriage was waiting for them and Zia told the coachman to take them to a large Emporium she had visited yesterday with the Dowager Marchioness.

While they had been shown around she had noticed there were a number of gowns for young girls which the Dowager Marchioness had not considered smart enough for her.

Zia was however well aware that Martha would look odd in anything too smart.

If she was to teach, as the Marquis had suggested, at the village School on his estate, she must not wear anything which would surprise or shock the villagers.

A footman had opened the door of the closed carriage.

The two girls got in but he waited for a moment after Zia had given him the address of the Emporium and looked back at the house.

"There is no one coming with us!" she exclaimed.

"You're goin' alone, Miss?"

"Just to the Emporium," Zia replied, "and it will not take long."

The footman shut the carriage door and they drove away.

"Are you quite sure you should do this?" Martha asked a little nervously. "I feel very strange dressed as I am now."

"You look very nice," Zia said, "and when you have clothes that really fit you, you will be surprised how attractive you will look!"

She knew as Martha looked away from her that she was feeling self-conscious about her plainness.

Zia told herself she had to try and give her confidence.

But that was definitely something that she would gain amongst the children who would not mind what she looked like as long as she was loving and understanding.

To take Martha's mind off herself Zia started to tell her about the Ball last night.

"What did the gentlemen say who danced with you?" Martha asked.

"They paid me a lot of compliments, and some of them looked at me with a 'swimmy' look in their eyes which I thought was rather ridiculous!" Zia replied.

"Did you dance with His Lordship?"

"He danced with me first, and he dances very well!" Zia replied.

Then she added:

"There was no one as handsome or smart as he was in the whole Ball-Room! Quite a lot of the lovely ladies in diamonds spoke to him in what I am sure my mother would have thought was an over-gushing manner."

"I expect they're in love with him!" Martha said.

Zia looked at her in surprise.

"Do you think so? But they were all married! I cannot remember their names, but one of them was a Countess, another a Duchess, and a third, who was very beautiful, was 'Lady something-or-other', and she said:

"'Rayburn, darling, when are you coming to see me?'"

"Did she really say that?" Martha asked.

Zia nodded.

"I thought at first she must be one of His Lordship's relatives, but as he moved away from her he just said:

"'That is the Countess of So-and-So, and a great number of people think she is the most beautiful woman in the whole of London!'"

"And was she?" Martha asked.

"I suppose she was," Zia replied. "She certainly made me feel rather plain and ordinary!"

"Oh, she couldn't have!" Martha exclaimed. "You're lovely, and the maids say you're the most beautiful person who has ever been at Oke House!"

"Did they really say that?" Zia asked with interest.

"They did! But they also said that the Lady Yasmin His Lordship's been meeting up to now is very beautiful."

Zia thought, then she said:

"I do not think anyone called Yasmin was there last night."

"No, she's in France," Martha explained. "I heard the Housekeeper tell Amy, the maid who looks after me, that her husband was very ill."

She thought for a moment, then she said:

"Lady Caton – that is what her name is – Yasmin Caton! And the way they talked it sounded as if His Lordship is infatuated with her."

Zia looked at her.

She had not until now thought of the Marquis as being infatuated with anybody.

Now she told herself she must be very stupid.

Of course, seeing how handsome he was, and how the lovely ladies had clustered round him last night should have made her aware that they were enamoured with him.

It was the same way, she thought now, that her mother had told her the ladies would sometimes pursue her father.

"You are too good-looking, darling!" she had said to him once, "and I am always afraid I shall lose you!"

"How could you possibly think anything like that?" the Colonel had replied. "There is not another woman as lovely as you in the world! From the moment I first saw you you stole my heart away, and I can assure you it is yours from now to eternity!"

Her mother had laughed and Zia remembered the expression of happiness there had been in her eyes.

She could picture now the way she had lifted her lips so that her father could kiss her.

"I want somebody to love me like that," she thought.

She knew it was something she could never feel towards any of the young men who had asked last night if they could call on her this afternoon.

At the same time, she knew she would have been very foolish not to realise how handsome, attractive and exciting the Marquis was.

"When I talked to him in the yacht," she thought, "I was not thinking of him as a man, but as if he was the Archangel Michael who had come down from Heaven to save me from the wickedness of Father Proteus."

She wondered what Lady Caton would have done if she had been in her place on the *Unicorn*.

Then before she could find a satisfactory answer they had arrived at the Emporium.

Zia had learnt quite a lot from the way the Dowager Marchioness had behaved.

She sent for the Manageress and said to her:

"I am Miss Langley who came here yesterday with the Dowager Machioness of Okehampton."

"Yes, yes, Miss, I remember it well," the Manageress replied.

"I have brought this young lady with me who is a friend of mine," Zia said indicating Martha, "and I want her dressed completely from head to foot. Her clothes have all been lost in an accident, and she has therefore nothing to wear but the dress I have lent her, which as you can see, does not fit her."

"Oh, dear, what a catastrophe!" the Manageress exclaimed. "But I am sure we can find what the young lady desires."

"Now, what she wants," Zia said firmly, "are clothes she can wear in the country which will not be ostentatious, if you understand what I mean. She is going to live very quietly helping a friend of His Lordship's to run a School."

As she spoke she saw by the expression on the Manageress's face that she understood exactly what she was trying to say to her.

"We have not much time," Zia went on, "and if we can have my friend fitted out with one or two gowns she can wear immediately, then the rest of the things can be sent as quickly as possible to Oke House."

It was an order which was exactly after the Manageress's heart.

In a very short while Martha was fitted out in a summer gown which was pretty but much plainer and less voluminous than the one Zia was wearing.

There was a hat to match it, and even shoes and stockings which came from another part of the Emporium.

Zia kept an eye on the clock, thinking perhaps the Dowager Marchioness might wish to do something with her before luncheon.

It was however getting on towards noon when they went outside to where the carriage was waiting.

Before they left the Manageress had promised to pack up everything they had chosen, and send it round to Oke House.

"Thank you very much!" Zia said to her as the footman got down from the box to open the door.

"It has been a pleasure, Miss, and I hope I shall see you here again," the Manageress replied.

"I am sure you will!" Zia smiled.

As she went through the Emporium door and out onto the pavement there was a wind blowing down the street and she put up her hand to hold onto her hat.

It prevented her from seeing anything but her way to the carriage, and she stepped inside it.

As she did so, the door was slammed to.

She looked back in astonishment to see Martha staggering then falling down on the pavement as if somebody had struck her.

But before she could see clearly what had occurred the horses started off, and she was aware that the footman who had slammed the door had now jumped up onto the box.

She could not understand what had occurred.

Then she looked through the glass window over the small seat which faced her.

She could see the coachman who was driving, and the footman sitting beside him.

She raised her hand to knock on the window to say they had left Martha behind.

As she did so the footman, wearing what she knew was the livery of the Marquis, turned round to look down at her.

It was then she saw his face and there was a scar which ran from his forehead into his eyebrow.

At the sight of him she gave a scream of horror and collapsed onto the back seat of the carriage.

Her heart was beating frantically with fear.

The footman looking at her was somebody she could not fail to recognise! He was Father Proteus's man – Saul!

Chapter Six

The Marquis, who had been riding with Harry, left him at the end of Park Lane.

"I will see you to-night," Harry said, "but now I have to hurry as I am having luncheon with the Duchess."

"She will be annoyed that you are late," the Marquis remarked.

"I know," Harry replied ruefully, "but it will be worth it to have had the best ride I have had for many a month!"

The Marquis was smiling as he trotted slowly up Park Lane towards his own house.

He was looking forward to seeing Zia, and hearing how she had enjoyed the Ball last night.

As his grandmother had said, she had been an undoubted success.

He thought it extraordinary that a girl who had lived such a sheltered life should step into the most sophisticated Society in Europe and manage to captivate everybody who saw her.

She was not shy, gauche, or anything else he might have expected a young girl to be.

"She is certainly original," he told himself, and knew that a lot of men were envying him for being her Guardian.

A groom was waiting for him outside the front door of Oke House, and dismounting he patted his horse as if to thank him for the ride.

Then he walked in through the front door which had been

opened by a footman.

To his astonishment he found the hall filled with people.

There was his secretary Mr. Barrett, the Housekeeper, his coachman and the footman peculiarly dressed, and several maidservants.

There was also a young woman in a pretty gown whom he did not recognise at once as being Sister Martha.

As he appeared they all stopped and stared at him in a way which told him without words that something was very wrong.

"What is it? What has happened?" he asked. "Why are you all here?"

He spoke to Mr. Barrett who exclaimed:

"Thank goodness you have returned, My Lord!"

"What is the matter?" the Marquis asked.

"Miss Zia has been kidnapped!"

For a moment the Marquis was too astonished to speak. Then he asked:

"When – and by whom?"

He knew the answer, but it was something he wanted to hear from the people staring at him.

His coachman, Dobson, a middle-aged man who had been with his father and was excellent with horses, came from among the crowd.

"It were loik this, M'Lord," he began, "t'weren't moi fault, nor Ben's . . ."

"Suppose you start at the beginning," the Marquis said quietly.

His voice was under control, and he appeared to be at ease.

At the same time his anger was rising, as he realised this was something he should have anticipated and prevented.

"I think you should know," Mr. Barrett interrupted, "that Miss Zia left the house soon after nine o'clock this morning, taking with her Sister Martha."

He glanced as he spoke at Martha who was standing near him with a handkerchief held to her eyes.

"Who else went with you?" the Marquis asked her.

"No one – My Lord."

"Where did you go?"

She took the handkerchief from her eyes to say:

"Zia came – into my – bedroom – and when I told her I was not – really a Nun – she said she would find me – the right clothes so that I – I could teach in the – School – Your Lordship spoke about."

Because she was sobbing as she spoke her words were almost incoherent, but the Marquis understood.

"So you went shopping alone in one of my carriages?"

"Y-yes, My Lord – then – Saul took her – away!"

As if the Marquis did not understand he looked at Dobson for a further explanation, and he said:

"When us reached t'Emporium, M'Lord, Miss Zia said as she'd be 'bout an hour-an'-half, so Oi takes t'horses under the shade o' th' trees in t'Square that's just be'oind Bond Street."

The Marquis nodded to show he understood and Dobson went on:

"Ben an' Oi were jus' sittin' talkin' in t'shade when we was suddenly hauled off th' box by two men, one o' them wi' a scar on 'is face."

"That was Saul!" Martha cried. "And he – hit me when I tried to get into – the carriage – with Zia!"

The Marquis ignored the interruption and said to Dobson:

"After they had pulled you from the carriage what did they do?"

"They took our coats an' 'ats, M'Lord, an' toid us up to a tree, then drove off with th' carriage!"

It seemed so incredible that for a moment the Marquis could only stare at his coachman.

Then Martha, as if she knew she must tell the rest of the story, moved a little nearer to him and said:

"We came out of – the shop and Zia got into the carriage – but when I would have joined her Saul – hit me so that I – fell down – then he jumped up – on the box and they – drove off."

She burst into tears as she said:

"Father Proteus – has her – again! Oh – save her – My Lord – save her!"

The Marquis looked at the other people in the hall.

"Has anybody anything to add to this story?" he asked.

There was no answer, and Mr. Barrett said:

"I think that is everything we know, My Lord."

"Very well!" the Marquis said. "Come with me, Barrett, and we will see what can be done. Everybody else can go back to their duties."

He walked towards the Study and Mr. Barrett followed him.

When his secretary shut the door the Marquis said:

"Has Her Ladyship been told about this?"

"Yes, My Lord, and she is very upset, and has therefore stayed in bed."

"That is sensible at any rate!" the Marquis said.

He sat down at his desk.

"Now, Barrett, what are we going to do?"

"I really have no idea, My Lord," Mr. Barrett replied, "except to send for the Police."

"If we do that," the Marquis said after a moment's pause, "the whole story will undoubtedly get into the newspapers."

Mr. Barrett said nothing.

The Marquis stared in front of him thinking furiously that Zia was again in the power of a dangerous man and somehow he had to save her.

He rose to walk to the window.

As he looked out with unseeing eyes at the sunshine in the garden, he felt as if his whole comfortable world had unexpectedly fallen about his ears.

Why had he not anticipated that Proteus instead of acknowledging defeat as he had expected, would not give up until he had Zia's money in his hands?

The Marquis was quite certain that this would now be a case of ransom, and Proteus was in a strong position to demand an outrageously large sum of money for the return of Zia.

He knew that what he had to do was to wait until the ransom note arrived.

Yet every nerve in his body was crying out for him to save Zia before she suffered any more than she must be already.

"Why did I not know? Why did I not guess," he asked himself, "that this might happen?"

He was furiously angry that he should have been so foolish as not to anticipate the way a criminal's mind would work.

"I have to do something!" the Marquis insisted.

But the only thing he could think was that London was a very large place.

If, as he suspected, Proteus intended to hide Zia until the money was in his hands, it would be completely impossible for anybody to find her.

He assumed that the false Priest would not play the same game again of hiding in a Convent or any other Religious Institution.

And yet he might have access to one whose doors were closed to the surveillance of the public.

What it all amounted to, the Marquis acknowledged to himself, was that he had no clue, no idea where Zia might be.

Later the horses and carriage might turn up.

But Proteus would take very good care that they were found far away from any secret place where he held Zia.

There was a note of despair in the Marquis's voice when after being silent for a long time he said:

"There must be something we can do!"

"That is what I have been telling myself, My Lord," Mr. Barrett replied. "Perhaps it would be possible to hire a Detective, or several of them, whom we could swear to secrecy."

"We will inevitably sooner or later have to call in the Police," the Marquis replied, "and I have no wish to do so, until Zia is safely home."

The way he spoke made Mr. Barrett aware that the Marquis was thinking that if the Police threatened Proteus he might in desperation, or perhaps revenge, kill his captive.

There was silence again, and, surprised at himself for doing so, the Marquis was actually praying that by some miracle he could gain an idea of where Zia had been taken.

The door opened and the Butler said:

"There's a man here, M'Lord, from the *Unicorn*, says his name's Winton, and he wishes to see Your Lordship, and I thinks, although I may be wrong, it concerns Miss Zia!"

The Marquis turned round quickly.

"Winton!" he exclaimed. "Send him in!"

As he waited he looked at Barrett, although neither of them said anything.

The Marquis was thinking that it was impossible that Winton could know anything.

His instructions after he had left the *Unicorn* were for it to proceed to Greenwich, where they were to wait until he required the yacht again.

It seemed to him now a long time, although it was actually only two or three minutes before Winton, who had called at the kitchen-door, came into the Study.

He was in uniform, but holding his cap in his hand.

He was looking somewhat over-awed until he saw the Marquis, then there was a grin on his face as he said:

"Good-day, M'Lord!"

"I understand you have something to tell me!" the Marquis said as if he could not waste any time.

"I 'ave, M'Lord!" Winton replied. "An' it be about Miss Langley."

The Marquis drew in his breath.

He walked to his desk, and indicated a chair on the other side of it before he said:

"Sit down, tell me everything you know!"

"Well, it's like this, M'Lord," Winton replied, sitting on the edge of his chair. "After yer Lordship left us, we moved the *Unicorn* a little way down river as th' Cap'an needed some vittles, an' he sends ashore for 'em. We also needed some paint, as yer Lordship'll remember, to touch up the yacht where t'was marked on th' starboard side."

"Yes, I remember," the Marquis said.

Only by a tremendous effort at self-control did he force himself not to shout at Winton to get to the point.

"Well – I were on deck, M'Lord," Winton went on, "seein' 'em urchins as was playin' about didn't make a nuisance of themselves when a little way down river I spots a man I'd seen afore."

"Who was it?" the Marquis asked. "And where had you seen him?"

"At th' Convent, M'Lord, the one yer took me to."

"You are sure that is where you saw him?"

"Yes, M'Lord. I sees him there lookin' out of t'window at me, an' I noticed him particular-like, 'cause he 'ad a scar on 'is forehead, running down into 'is eyebrow, it was!"

"Yes, yes!" the Marquis said. "His name is Saul."

"I sees 'im again," Winton went on, "when 'e runs out of th' gate as we were leavin' with Miss Langley, an' yer Lordship tells I to fire th' pistol over their 'eads."

Winton paused for breath and the Marquis said:

"And you saw him again to-day on the river?"

"Yes, M'Lord. 'Im an' another man was climbing into a boat as was bein' rowed by two others."

"A boat!" the Marquis exclaimed.

"Yes, M'Lord."

"And they were alone?"

"No, M'Lord. They 'ad a woman with 'em. I couldn't see her clearly, not then, but . . ."

"Go on!" the Marquis said impatiently.

"'Cause I were curious, M'Lord, I leaves Harper – yer knows Harper, M'Lord?"

"Yes, yes," the Marquis answered. "Go on with what you were saying."

"I walks down to see where they was a-goin' an' as they gets into mid-stream I recognises th' lady as is with 'em – it were Miss Langley, M'Lord!"

"You are quite sure?" Mr. Barrett asked as if he could keep silent no longer.

Winton turned towards Mr. Barrett.

"Yes, Sir, I were quite sure it be Miss Langley. She 'ad no 'at on 'er 'ead so I could see 'er quite clear-like."

"You watched them?" the Marquis asked. "Where did they go?"

"They goes straight across th' river, M'Lord, downstream a short way, then into an 'ouse-boat."

"You are quite certain it was a house-boat?"

"Oh, yes, M'Lord, an' there was only one at that partic'lar point on th' river, lyin' by some bushes, an' a pretty tumbledown affair it be an' all, needin' paint. Not the sort o' boat as yer Lordship'd give a second glance to!"

"A house-boat!" the Marquis exclaimed. "And that is where Miss Langley is now?"

"They takes 'er ashore, M'Lord, an' I were certain that after that they takes 'er aboard."

The Marquis put his hand to his head as if it helped him to think more clearly.

"You have done me a great service, Winton, for which you will be amply rewarded," he said. "Now I want you to have something to eat while I talk to Mr. Barrett and decide how we will rescue Miss Langley."

As he rose to his feet Winton rose too, then he said:

"Yer'll let me in on it, M'Lord? You knows I can be trusted with a pistol . . ."

"I promise you shall be in on it," the Marquis said. "Just give me time to work out my plan of campaign."

Mr. Barrett had already rung the bell for him and the door opened almost immediately.

"See that Winton is given something substantial to eat," the Marquis said to the Butler, "and I will send for him a little later."

"Very good, M'Lord!"

The Marquis did not say any more until Winton had left the room.

He was telling himself that, incredibly, his prayer had been answered, and by a miracle he knew where Zia was.

Zia was very frightened.

She had been terrified when the carriage had driven away with her from the Emporium and she knew she had been captured by Father Proteus's men.

She tried to think of some way that she could throw herself out of the carriage.

But the horses were travelling as fast as they could in the traffic and she was certain if she did try to get out she would fall under the wheels.

Even if she was not injured, Saul would catch her before she could run away, and he might then hit her as he had just hit Martha.

Sitting on the back seat and supporting herself because they were travelling so fast, she thought how stupid she had been to go shopping with Martha without taking anybody with them.

Then she thought that even if the Housekeeper or a maid had come with them, they would have been powerless to prevent her from being carried away.

In some frightening manner the Marquis's coachman and footman had been disposed of, and Saul and another of

Father Proteus's men were now driving the carriage.

She sat trembling, realising they had left the shops behind and were entering a poorer and dirtier part of the City.

She caught a sudden glimpse of water and realised the Thames was just ahead of them.

She had the terrifying feeling that Father Proteus was going to take her away in a ship to a foreign country.

If he did that she knew that no one would ever find her again – not even the Marquis.

As she thought of him her whole being cried out towards him to save her.

He had saved her once, and she remembered how exciting it had been as he had driven her away from the Convent and she thought she was rid of Father Proteus for ever.

At the back of her mind she had always been afraid that she would never escape.

Now she was back in his clutches, and she knew he would never be satisfied until he had control of, if not all her money, then a great deal of it.

"What can I do?" she asked.

Then she was praying to the Marquis to come once again to her rescue.

"Save . . . me! Save . . . me," she cried in her heart, "as . . . only . . . you can . . . do!"

The carriage came to a standstill and she realised they were on a road which bordered the river.

She wondered if she jumped out and threw herself into the Thames whether she would be able to escape.

She could swim because her father had taught her, but she knew it would be very difficult in the full-skirted gown she was wearing.

She was more likely to sink and be drowned.

The door of the carriage was pulled open and Saul was leering at her with an evil expression in his eyes under the scar which disfigured his forehead.

"Come on!" he said. "You've 'ad a nice ride, an' now we're taking you on th' water!"

Zia realised it was no use arguing with him.

As he spoke he was pulling off the livery coat he had obviously taken from the Marquis's servants, and he flung it into the carriage.

The coachman, whom she recognised as a man who had been at the Convent and who was called Mark, threw his after it.

Then the two men in their shirt-sleeves each took one of her arms and marched her down to the water's edge.

As they did so she heard the carriage drive away and hoped that whoever had taken it would be kind to the Marquis's fine horses.

Then she saw below her there was a rowing-boat in which the other two men who had been at the Convent were waiting.

"'Ere she be!" Saul said to them. "An' a good deal more fancy t' look at than when we last sees 'er!"

He pushed Zia into the boat, then the two men who were already in it started to row across the river.

There was a strong current and Zia wondered if they would be swept away and whether if the boat capsized perhaps she would have a chance of escaping.

With a great deal of puffing and blowing they managed to reach calmer waters and she saw ahead of them what appeared to be a very dilapidated house-boat.

It was moored to a rough bank and at first she could not believe that was their destination.

Then as they pulled the boat to the bank and dragged her out onto the rough ground, she knew that this improbable hiding-place was where she was to be imprisoned.

For a moment she thought of screaming and shouting and making one desperate dash for freedom.

Then as she looked at the rough, unbuilt-on ground against which the house-boat was moored she saw this was a lonely spot where there were no wharfs and in consequence few people.

If she screamed who would hear her?

If anyone did, who was likely to confront Saul and Mark and the other two men who looked as tough and pugnacious as they were?

But she had, as it happened, little time for thought.

The men pulled her up the very rickety gang-plank and onto the deck, taking her through a dilapidated door into what she supposed was the Saloon.

Sitting in an armchair, his leg in a splint, was Father Proteus, a bottle of brandy beside him.

At the sight of him, Zia felt herself shiver.

She knew as she looked at him how furious he was that she had escaped.

"'Ere she be!" Saul said brightly.

"You've been a devil of a long time!" Father Proteus complained. "Does anyone know you've brought her here?"

"Not unless they're birds in the sky!" Saul replied. "An' Dixon's taken off the 'orses."

"What has he done with them?" Father Proteus asked.

"'E'll sell 'em soon as 'e gets the chance, an' put the carriage in a Scrap-yard."

Zia shut her eyes.

She thought of how the Marquis would mind his horses, of which he was so proud, being sold to some buyer who might over-work them, or worse, be cruel to them.

Then as Father Proteus' eyes were on her she could only think of herself.

"A fine dance you've led me, my girl!" he said as he glared at her. "But you'll pay for it, just as you'll pay for that damnable Guardian of yours cracking up my leg!"

He shouted the words at her. Then as if he hated the very sight of her he said:

"Take her below and lock her in! Take away her gown and shoes just in case she tries to escape."

"Her won't be able t'do that!" Saul said.

He was laughing at the idea, and Zia knew he was gloating over the fact that she was helpless, and there was nothing she could do about it.

He had seized Zia by the arm, digging his fingers into the softness of her skin.

"Now listen," Father Proteus said as if a sudden thought struck him, "you are going to write a letter to your Guardian, telling him that unless he pays every penny I ask of him, I'll kill you – do you understand?"

With an effort Zia managed to say defiantly:

"If you kill me as you killed that other girl at the Convent you will be hanged!"

Father Proteus laughed, and it was a very unpleasant sound.

"Do you suppose I am as stupid as you are?" he asked. "If we put you in the Thames and hold your head down, you'll float away on the tide and be many miles from here before somebody pulls your dead, limp body out of the water!"

The way he spoke made Zia feel as if she must scream and go on screaming, but with a superhuman effort she pressed her lips together and said nothing.

"Take her away!" Father Proteus ordered. "It makes me sick to look at her!"

Saul dragged Zia towards the door and Father Proteus roared:

"Mark – bring another bottle of brandy! This damned leg is hurting like all the fires of Satan!"

Saul pulled Zia down the companionway, the steps of which were cracked and broken, to the lower deck of the house-boat.

There was a passage with several doors opening out of it which she knew were the cabins.

He took her to one near the stern which looked out onto the river.

She knew it was because he had no intention of letting her think she might climb through a porthole onto dry land.

He stood for a moment looking round the very small cabin.

As if he wanted to hurt her, he gave her a push in the middle of her back that sent her sprawling onto a narrow iron bedstead which stood in the centre of it.

"Now you be'ave yerself," he warned, "or I promise ye, you'll suffer worse than 'His Nibs' be!"

It was a threat which instinctively made Zia cringe away from him.

He laughed, and it was a harsh sound that seemed to echo round the small cabin, then he left.

She heard him close the door and lock it, and she had the idea that it was a new lock that had been specially put there to keep her from escaping.

Just as she thought she was rid of him, she heard the key turn again and he came back.

"Yer 'eard wot the Old Man said!" he leered. "Give us yer dress and yer shoes!"

"I will put them outside the door when I have taken them off!" Zia replied.

"Shy, are ye?" Saul sniggered. "I'll 'elp yer, if ye can't manage."

"Wait outside the door!" Zia said.

She spoke firmly, looking at him defiantly, and for one terrifying moment she thought he would not do as she said.

Then, as if he felt it was a mistake to molest her, he went from the cabin and she knew he was waiting outside.

Quickly, because she was afraid he might come back in again and touch her, she took off the beautiful gown she had put on to go shopping with Martha.

As it fell to the floor she picked it up with her shoes and opening the door as short a way as possible handed them through.

She saw Saul's dirty hands come out to take them.

"Ye can 'ave this back when ye've paid for it!" he jeered.

She slammed the door to – as he laughed.

Once again the key was turned in the lock and Zia sank down on the bed feeling that she must be the most frightened person in the whole world.

Not even the Marquis would be able to find her, and she was in the power of men who would not hesitate to kill her if it would save their skins.

She wanted to beat on the wall, to cry despairingly, but her sixth sense told her that would be no help.

Somehow, and she was not even certain why, she knew she had to keep her wits about her.

She went to the porthole to look out on the river.

The Thames was very wide at this particular point and she could see on the other side of the river there were only wharfs and industrial buildings, but no houses for human habitation.

Even if I were able to signal, she thought, nobody would be there to see it, and Saul and the other men would not hesitate to attack me if they knew what I was doing.

She went from the porthole to sit on the bed.

It contained an old faded mattress from which the stuffing was escaping in a number of places, and the cover was torn and stained.

There were two thin blankets, which were also none too clean.

Otherwise the cabin was empty and looked as if it had been so for a long time.

"I could die here and nobody would be aware of it!" Zia said to herself.

Then almost as if a voice told her so, she knew that her father and mother would know and, whatever else happened, they would never forget her.

"Help me . . . Papa," she prayed. "You have been in . . . dangerous situations in your life . . . but I never thought it would . . . happen to . . . me!"

Then once again she knew the only person who could save her was the Marquis.

He had saved her from the Convent when she had thought she was utterly lost and forgotten.

She was quite certain that when Father Proteus had got hold of her money as he intended, she would die in some strange accident which no one could prove was murder.

Father Proteus would also wish to kill her because he blamed her for being instrumental in injuring his leg.

She was sure that when he had threatened her with drowning, he was already planning that was what he would do once her money was in his hands.

She started to pray again; praying to her father, her mother, and the Marquis.

"Save me . . . save . . . me!"

It was a cry that not only came from her heart but her soul.

It was late in the day, and outside the sun was sinking as Zia heard footsteps coming below.

She had heard the voices of the men, although they had not been talking noisily for fear of drawing attention to themselves.

Now the key turned in the lock and when the door opened it was Mark who stood there.

He had a tray in his hand and she saw that on it was food of some sort and a cup and saucer.

He put the tray down on the end of the bed and said:

"Father Proteus says – although he ain't a Father no longer – us've got to keep yer alive 'til yer've write a letter for yer money, so eat up, otherwise one of us'll have to feed yer!"

He waited for Zia to reply, and when she said nothing he went on:

"Sulky, are ye? Well, us'll 'ave to think o' some way o' cheerin' yer up, won't we?"

He gave her a look which made her shiver, then he went from the cabin locking the door after him.

She looked at the food on the tray thinking she was really too frightened and unhappy to be hungry.

There were some slices of cold meat which did not look at all appetising on a cracked plate, and a piece of bread from a cottage loaf which had obviously been newly baked.

To eat with it on the same plate as the meat was a pat of butter, and a piece of rather evil-smelling cheese.

In the cup was some coffee which at least smelt fragrant.

She remembered then how Father Proteus when he was at the Convent drank a great deal of coffee, and she knew if nothing else this at least would be drinkable.

She ate a little of the bread and butter, but drank all the coffee.

Then she put the tray down near the door so that whoever fetched it would not have to come far into the cabin.

By now it was dusk and a little while later she heard a sound which at first terrified her.

Then she realised the men were carrying Father Proteus down the rickety companionway to a cabin not far from hers.

Whenever they hurt his leg with the movements they made he swore oaths she had never heard before, but was quite certain were lewd and vulgar.

She also had the idea from the sound of the men's voices that they had all had a great deal to drink.

Because she was frightened they might come to see her she held her breath and her whole body was tense until she heard Saul say:

"Now yer knows what ye've got to do. We all sleeps up top, an' Mark an' Mike'll take th' first watch while Joseph and me takes th' second."

"I'm sleepy!" she heard Mark complain.

"Yer'd better not let th' Old Man hear ye say that!" Saul replied.

The other man, Joseph, said something unpleasant which made them all laugh, then they climbed up on deck and Zia gave a sigh of relief.

She supposed she should try to sleep.

To-morrow when she had to write the letter to ask for the ransom she might be able, if she was clever, to put some clue in it as to where she was being held.

Then she knew despairingly that whatever she wrote would be read and re-read by Father Proteus to be quite certain she had not betrayed them.

"Help me . . . Papa . . . help me!" she prayed.

Then she thought again of the Marquis.

She felt as if she could see him as he had looked last night: so smart, so handsome, so irresistible to all the ladies who had clustered round him.

Then she remembered how she had danced with him and how exciting it had been to be close to him with his hand on her waist.

"If only he was . . . here . . . now!" she whispered.

As she spoke her heart throbbed, a little thrill ran through her.

Then she knew that she loved him, and had done so ever since they had been together on the yacht.

The Marquis had made his plans very carefully.

He was desperately afraid however that if anything went wrong Zia might be hurt.

As he drove down to the river with Winton in his closed carriage his mind was working like a well-oiled machine, to make certain he had thought of every possible detail.

When he went aboard the *Unicorn* he had called the Captain and the crew into the Saloon.

He told them what had happened and what he had decided to do. He then went on:

"We are not dealing with ordinary criminals, but extremely clever ones. One slip, one mistake, and we shall fail to rescue Miss Langley."

"I assure you, My Lord," the Captain said, "your orders will be carried out, and as you well know, several of the men aboard the *Unicorn* have served in the Navy."

"I know that," the Marquis said, "and I am relying on them, Captain, as I am on you, to help me save Miss Zia from men who every one of them should be behind bars, while the head of the gang should undoubtedly be hanged!"

The Marquis then stayed aboard the *Unicorn* until one-thirty in the morning.

Silently, leaving only two of the older members of the crew to keep watch, the rest set out.

Each man was aware of his part in a plan of attack which they all recognised could only have been thought out by someone as clever as the Marquis.

Six of the seamen landed up-river, some distance from the house-boat, and well out of sight.

They approached the house-boat singly, moving through the unbuilt-on ground where there were a number of rough bushes which afforded a certain amount of cover.

When they were near the house-boat, Winton and another man crawled forward cautiously, making no sound so that the two men on watch on the house-boat had no idea of their presence.

Saul and Joseph were in fact not only inebriated but also sleepy.

They had gone up on deck as they had been told to do.

Saul was sitting down near the gang-plank with his back against the wall of the Saloon and his eyes kept closing.

Joseph in the bow of the ship had lain down on deck, and was so drunk as to be almost unconscious.

Neither of the so-called guards was aware that Winton and the man with him had cut the ropes which held the house-boat to the bank.

Creeping along the muddy side of the river up to their knees in water, four other seamen started to push the house-boat down stream.

The tide was going out and it was easy with their combined strength to move the boat away from the bank in what at first was only a few feet of water.

Then as it was caught by the current, it swung out at about ten feet from dry land.

It was then that Winton, standing up, shouted:

"Hi, Mister! Yer boat's afloat!"

His voice aroused Saul who looked up, saw a dark figure on the bank, and for some seconds could not realise what was happening.

Then Winton said:

"Throw us yer rope an' I'll pull ye back!"

As Winton was shouting two other seamen came to his side, and Saul's cries for help brought Mark, Joseph and Jacob to assist him.

Nobody noticed in the dark that the seamen from the yacht were dripping wet below the waist.

They were too intent on throwing the ropes which were lying in the stern of the house-boat onto the shore.

It was extraordinary how difficult it seemed to be, and how clumsy Winton and the other two men with him were at catching the ropes.

They seemed to slip through their hands so that they had to be thrown again and again.

Winton was joined by more men making six, also wet, but they were no more successful than the others.

The noise of the men shouting: "'Ere, catch this!" "Look out!" "'Ere's another!" seemed to fill the air.

As the Marquis swam to the other side of the house-boat, he was quite sure that nobody would notice him.

He knew that Zia would be locked in one of the cabins, and he wasted no time by looking through the port-holes.

Instead, he climbed with the expertise of an athlete up the side of the rickety house-boat and onto the deck which faced the Thames.

No one was there to see him.

He went to the door on the opposite side to where the men were shouting at each other and slipped down the companionway.

Although it was dark, he managed by the lights that had been left burning in the Saloon to see the cabin doors.

He felt with his hands the first one he came to, realising as he tried the handle that the door was unlocked, and moved quickly away.

He could hear somebody shouting in one cabin and knew it was Father Proteus.

He was calling for one of his men to come and tell him what was happening.

Then the Marquis's hand encountered a strong lock and a key, and he knew he had found who he was seeking.

He turned the key and opened the door.

Zia, who had been aroused by all the noise, was sitting up against the back of the bed.

For a moment, as the door opened and she saw the shadow of a man, she thought it was Saul.

She was so frightened that although she opened her mouth to scream, no sound came.

Then her instinct told her who it was.

As the Marquis's arms went out towards her, she threw herself against him and put her arms around his neck like a child who had been frightened by the dark.

"It is . . . you . . . !" she managed to say.

Then his lips were on hers to silence the words.

As he kissed her she felt as if the sky had opened and a light enveloped them both. Her whole body seemed to come alive.

Then when the Marquis picked her up in his arms, she realised he was wet through and knew how he had reached her.

Yet she held herself close against him as he carried her up the companionway, and out onto the deck which faced the river.

"You are quite safe," he whispered, "there is a boat below."

As he lowered her down the side strong arms reached up to take her from him.

The boat was manned by three seamen, and as the Marquis got into it, he joined Zia in the stern, and they pulled away from the house-boat.

He put his arm around her to hold her against him, and because she felt he had lifted her up to Heaven, she hid her face against his wet shoulder.

He did not speak and they were half-way across the Thames before he said:

"You are safe, and this shall never happen to you again!"

She did not answer, but he could feel her quivering against him.

As she did so he vowed to himself to protect her, to keep her safe, and to love her for the rest of his life.

"How can I have been such a fool as to lose her?" he had asked himself a thousand times while he and his crew were waiting to go into action.

Now he had won a victory, but the only thing that mattered was that Zia was with him again.

Chapter Seven

As the rowing-boat reached the river bank unexpectedly the clouds rolled away.

It had been a dark night, but now the moon was shining and as the Marquis picked up Zia in his arms and carried her off the boat he looked back.

He could see now more clearly than he had been able to do before that the house-boat had drifted almost to the middle of the river.

It was dipping heavily at the stern, and he knew it was filling with water.

On his orders, the seamen who had pushed it away from the bank had, once he had rowed away with Zia, made a hole just below the water level.

He was sure it would not be a difficult thing to do because the boat was so dilapidated.

Now he knew the stern was taking in water and he thought already it must be deep in the cabin where Proteus was.

He could see quite clearly his own men on the bank and the four men of the gang on the house-boat must have jumped overboard and were struggling to reach land.

Two were coming out of the water, and would be seized by his men as soon as they landed.

The other two were in difficulties, and he suspected they could not swim.

If they were to drown as well as Father Proteus, it would be a good thing, and would save any Court proceedings which would be brought against them by the Police.

The Marquis's carriage was waiting and having deposited Zia on the back seat, he stood for a moment looking again at the house-boat.

Now it was definitely sinking, and he was sure it was only a question of time, perhaps five or ten minutes, before it sank altogether.

That meant that Proteus could never threaten Zia again.

He climbed into the carriage and as a footman put a rug over his knees he realised that Zia had crossed her hands over her breasts.

For the first time he was aware that she was wearing only a silk chemise and her petticoat.

Very gently he wrapped the rug around her like a shawl.

Then as the carriage moved off she looked up at him and said in a lilting voice:

"You . . . saved . . . me!"

He put his arm around her and replied:

"You are safe, my darling, and I shall never forgive myself for not anticipating that this might happen."

"I prayed that . . . you would save me . . . and I am sure Papa . . . helped you to . . . do so."

"I am sure he did," the Marquis replied, "but all that matters for the moment is that you are safe."

He pulled her a little closer to him, then he said:

"I am afraid I have made you wet."

"It does not matter," Zia said. "I just want to be quite sure you are here."

She put her hand on his shoulder as if to reassure herself, and he said gently:

"There is a better way of making sure."

As he spoke his lips came down on hers.

To Zia it was what she had wanted and what she had been longing for.

She had been afraid when they were in the boat that he had kissed her merely to prevent her from speaking.

Now sensations she had never known before were rippling through her body, and she felt her love rising up towards him almost like the waves of the sea.

"I love you . . . I love you!" she wanted to say, but it was impossible to speak.

As the Marquis kissed her and went on kissing her with slow, passionate kisses it made her feel as if she was part of him and they could never be separated.

All she knew was that it was as if a blinding light from Heaven surrounded them both, and it made her quiver with the intensity of it.

She had the strange feeling that the Marquis felt the same.

They had driven a long way before he said:

"Because I do not want you ever again to be worried as I know you are at this moment, the man you called 'Proteus' has been drowned!"

There was a little pause as if Zia found it hard to think of anything except the ecstasy he had given her.

Then she asked in a low voice:

"In the . . . house-boat?"

"There was nothing to prevent it from sinking to the bottom of the river," the Marquis said.

Zia drew in her breath.

"Perhaps it is . . . wrong to . . . be glad . . . but now I need . . . no longer be . . . afraid."

"That is something you will never be again," the Marquis said, "and to make sure of it, how soon will you marry me, my precious?"

They were passing some lights and as she looked up at him he could see the expression of radiance on her face.

Then as he waited, once again she hid her face against his shoulder.

"You . . . cannot really want to . . . marry me!" she said in a low voice.

"I want it more than I have ever wanted anything in my life before," the Marquis replied, "and, darling, no one can accuse me of being a fortune-hunter!"

"I . . . I was not thinking of that," Zia said, "but perhaps I will . . . bore . . . you and you would be . . . happier with one of the . . . beautiful ladies I saw at the . . . Ball."

It was only then, and it seemed extraordinary that he should have forgotten her, that the Marquis remembered Yasmin.

He knew this was the solution that Harry had suggested.

But he could honestly swear, although no one would believe him, that in his anxiety to find Zia and rescue her from Proteus, he had never given a thought to his own problem of Yasmin's allegations.

Now he knew that to marry Zia provided a genuine and uncontrived answer, but she must never be aware of the predicament he had been in.

Because it was easier to convince her how much he wanted her by kisses rather than words, he kissed her until they arrived back at Oke House.

As the horses came to a standstill Zia said:

"We are . . . home!"

"That is what it will be to you in the future," the Marquis said.

Then as a footman opened the door of the carriage, Zia gave a little cry.

"What is it?" the Marquis asked.

"I have forgotten . . . I have forgotten to tell you what has happened to your horses!"

The door was open, but he did not move and she knew he was listening.

"A man called Dixon collected them from the river bank, and he is going to . . . sell them!"

137

There was a little tremor in Zia's voice because she knew how much it would upset the Marquis.

"The carriage," she added, "is to be taken to the . . . scrap-yards."

"Thank you, my darling," the Marquis said quietly, and got out of the carriage.

As he went into the house he was not surprised to find his secretary waiting for him.

"I have brought Miss Langley home, Barrett," he said, "and I have some important instructions to give you."

Mr. Barrett waited and the Marquis picked Zia up in his arms.

"I am carrying you," he said, "because I think you have been through enough for one night, and the sooner you go to bed and dream of me, the better!"

As he started up the stairs she smiled up at him.

"I shall dream of . . . you," she said, "and keep . . . thanking you . . . over and over again in . . . my heart."

He did not answer, but carried her down the corridor and into her bedroom where the lights were lit.

There was no maid waiting, but the Marquis knew he had only to pull the bell and she would come at once.

Very gently he put Zia down on the bed, then holding her close against him kissed her fiercely and possessively.

"You are mine!" he said. "We will talk about it tomorrow."

She looked at him, her eyes shining, and the Marquis thought no woman could look more lovely or desirable.

With an effort he turned towards the door.

"Please . . . change your clothes at once!" Zia cried. "I am afraid you may catch a chill."

The Marquis was wearing just a shirt and a pair of tight-fitting black trousers.

They were not as wet as they had been, but they were still damp, and he knew that Zia was being sensible.

"I will do as you tell me," he said as he went from the room, "which of course I will always do in the future!"

She laughed because she knew it was she who would be obeying him, which was only what she wanted to do.

Then before she pulled the bell for her maid, she knelt down beside the bed.

Fervently she thanked God that she was safe and that Father Proteus could never hurt her again.

Zia had gone to sleep hoping that what hours were left of the night would pass quickly so that she could see the Marquis again.

In fact she slept peacefully until noon.

When she awoke she rang for her breakfast, but before it could arrive, Martha came into her room.

"You are back! Thank God you are back!" she exclaimed. "Oh, Zia, we have all been so frightened for you!"

"I am safe, thanks to His Lordship," Zia smiled, "but Martha, it was very, very frightening!"

"It must have been," Martha agreed, "but we have all had strict instructions from His Lordship not to speak about it to you, to each other, or to anybody else!"

Zia was surprised, then when she thought it over she knew that the Marquis was wise.

If what had happened was talked about in the house it would certainly soon be gossiped about by his smart friends, and then it might appear in the newspapers.

Father Proteus is dead! she thought to herself, and the sooner everybody . . . forgets about . . . him the . . . better!

Martha was however saying how frightened everybody had been, and before the Marquis arrived back Dobson had been in tears over the loss of his horses.

"I have just heard from Mr. Barrett," Martha went on, "that the horses have been found and brought back to His Lordship's stables."

"I am so glad!" Zia said. "I could not bear such magnificent animals to be hurt or sold to somebody who was cruel to them."

"They too are safe," Martha smiled, "and now Mr. Barrett is thinking of taking me to the country next week to meet the lady who teaches at the School."

Because she sounded so excited about it, Zia changed the conversation from herself to Martha's new career and her new clothes.

All she really wanted however was to see the Marquis, and when she was dressed she ran downstairs to find out if he was in the house.

She found him in the Study and when she opened the door he was alone.

When he saw her he rose from his desk and moving to one side of it held out his arms.

She ran towards him and he pulled her close to him and kissed her until they were both breathless.

"I was afraid you might have disappeared once again!" he said in his deep voice.

"No, I am here, and when I woke up I was sure I was dreaming."

He kissed her again before he drew her towards the sofa and they both sat down.

"I have been making a lot of arrangements," he said. "First I went to see the Archbishop at Lambeth Palace, and arrived there just as he was finishing his breakfast."

Zia looked at him wide-eyed and he explained:

"He has given me a Special Licence, and that means, my lovely one, that we can go to Oke Castle and be married tomorrow, soon after we arrive, by my Chaplain."

"M-married!" Zia whispered.

"I want you with me both by day and by *night*," the Marquis said emphasizing the last word.

Zia blushed and he thought she looked as beautiful as dawn breaking over the sky.

"I am not going to wait a minute longer," he said. "Such unpredictable and extraordinary things happen to you that I am taking no more chances!"

"I want to marry you . . . I want to be . . . your wife," Zia whispered, "and it will be . . . very . . . very wonderful for me!"

"And for me!" the Marquis said.

He kissed her again, and they only moved apart hastily when the door opened and Harry came in.

"Good morning!" he said cheerily. "What has been happening? Zia never turned up at the party last night, and you, Rayburn, failed to come riding with me this morning!"

"I am sorry, Harry," the Marquis said, "but I have in fact been very busy. First I want you to congratulate me, because Zia has promised to become my wife!"

"That is the best news I have heard in years!" Harry said. "Congratulations, old boy! And may I kiss your future bride?"

"Just this once," the Marquis said grudgingly, "but I do not expect you to make a habit of it!"

Harry laughed and kissed Zia on both cheeks.

Then as if he could not resist it, the Marquis said:

"We will tell you what happened, but you must never relate it to a living soul!"

"I knew something was up!" Harry said. "Give me a glass of champagne to fortify myself before I hear the tale."

He settled himself in an armchair with a glass of champagne in his hand, listening in astonishment to the story the Marquis unfolded to him.

Only when it was ended did he realise that his glass of champagne had remained untouched and he exclaimed:

"I just cannot believe it! All I have to say, Rayburn, is that I will never forgive you for not letting me in on the rescue-party!"

"I visited the *Unicorn* this morning," the Marquis remarked, "and I have never seen men so elated and pleased with themselves. Actually there were only three men to take to the Police Station, where they have now been charged."

He glanced at Zia before he said a little hastily, in case it should upset her:

"The man who called himself Father Proteus was drowned, and so was Saul, otherwise they would both have been charged with murder. However the others have not been charged with kidnapping, but only with stealing valuable relics from the Convent."

"That was clever of you!" Harry approved.

"They have been forced to reveal the whereabouts of the loot, and they will get several years imprisonment for theft."

"So that disposes of everything that was menacing," Harry said.

His eyes met the Marquis's and they both knew that he was referring to Yasmin Caton.

They all had luncheon together and talked of everything except the horror that Zia had been put through.

After luncheon was over, the Marquis said:

"I still have a great deal to do, and as you will appreciate, my darling, the one person I must let into the secret that we are being married tomorrow night is the Prince of Wales. He would be very hurt if like everybody else he learnt of it the day after tomorrow in *The Gazette*."

"And we are going to the country!" Zia said quickly.

She wanted to avoid meeting the beautiful ladies who had pursued the Marquis, and who now would be upset because he was married.

Because they would be jealous, she was sure they would make subtle remarks to him about her which might make the Marquis love her less.

"We will leave soon after breakfast," the Marquis promised, "and now I want you to rest, as Grandmama is doing, until tea-time."

The Dowager Marchioness had been thrilled to learn that her grandson had found Zia and that she was safe.

She had been so upset at what had happened that she had been advised to stay in bed, although she had said firmly that she would be down for dinner.

"I will look forward to seeing you then, Grandmama," the Marquis had said, "when I will tell you why I am the happiest man in the world!"

When he left her the Dowager Marchioness shed a few tears because she too was happy.

She had loved her grandson ever since he was a small boy.

She had regretted bitterly as the years passed that while there was a succession of beautiful women in his life, she had felt that with each *affaire de coeur* he became more and more cynical.

Now there was a happiness about him she had never known.

She felt her prayers had been answered because Zia was exactly the right wife for him.

Because she was too excited and happy to be tired Zia did not go to her room to rest.

Instead she went to the Marquis's Study so that when he returned she would not miss a moment of his company.

She took a book from the case to read, but in fact she sat thinking how wonderful he was, and that no one else could be more fortunate than herself because he loved her.

Then when she was praying that she would never fail him the door opened and she heard Carter the Butler say:

"As you see, M'Lady, I'm not deceiving you, and His Lordship's not here."

"Then I will wait until he returns," a woman's voice said.

"Very good, M'Lady," Carter replied in a somewhat exasperated tone.

Zia was aware as he shut the door that she was no longer alone.

She had been sitting in a deep armchair beside the fireplace which was hidden from the door, and now a little nervously she rose to her feet.

Standing by the desk was one of the most beautiful women she had ever seen.

Dressed in black, she was nevertheless extremely elegant, with a bustle larger than anything the Dowager Marchioness would have let her buy.

As Zia hesitated, wondering what she should say, the Lady, who had been staring at a pile of letters, turned her head and saw her.

As she did so she stiffened, and there was no mistaking the hostile expression in her eyes.

"You are Zia Langley, I suppose!" she said in a hard voice.

"Y-yes . . . I am," Zia answered, "and if you are waiting for His Lordship, I am afraid he will be away for some time."

"Then I will speak to you!" Lady Caton replied. "I have heard, although it may be untrue, that His Lordship intends to marry you."

"It is to be announced the day after tomorrow."

Yasmin Caton gave a shrill scream.

"Then it *is* true! When I heard the rumour I was sure it must be a lie, because no man – no man in the whole world – could behave so despicably, so disgracefully! I only wish I could kill him for it!"

She spoke so violently that Zia was frightened.

"What . . . are you . . . saying? I . . . I do not . . . understand!"

"Then let me tell you what you ought to know," the woman said moving a little nearer to her. "I am Lady Caton and the Marquis, with whom I suppose you fancy yourself to be in love, is a man of no principles, no decency!

He is marrying you merely to escape from his responsibilities."

She seemed to spit the words at Zia who instinctively moved back a step or two.

"I . . . I do not . . . understand what . . . you are saying."

"The truth is that Rayburn was in love with me. Because I believed his protestations of affection I became his mistress, and he promised that as soon as my husband died he would marry me!"

Her voice sharpened as she went on:

"Now that I am free, he has run away from me and from the child I carry which is his."

For a few seconds Zia did not understand what she was saying, then when she did she went very pale.

"You . . . you are . . . having . . . a . . . baby?" she stammered.

"I suppose you can understand English?" Yasmin Caton snapped. "Yes, I am carrying the Marquis's child, and are you prepared, you stupid little rich girl, who will bore him stiff within a few weeks, to let him hide behind your skirts rather than do what is right and make my child legitimate?"

Zia could only stare at her. At the same time, she was trembling.

Then suddenly, as if she wished to intimidate her, Yasmin Caton said:

"Go away! Leave him alone! He is mine – do you understand? He is mine, and however hard he tries to, I will not let him leave me!"

She spoke so violently that her voice echoed round the Study.

With a cry like that of a small, hurt animal, Zia turned and ran from the room.

She ran along the passage, across the hall, unaware that Carter and the footmen were staring at her, and up the stairs.

She rushed into her bed-room and shutting the door flung herself down on the bed.

She was so shocked, so stunned by what she had heard that she could not even cry.

She only lay there feeling as if the beautiful woman who betrayed the Marquis had stabbed her in a thousand places and her whole body was bleeding to death.

"I have . . . to go . . . away!" she thought. "She . . . is right, and if she is . . . bearing his . . . child . . . he must . . . marry her!"

Then she thought she had nowhere to go.

There must be somewhere, but she could not think of it.

Then almost as if she was being helped, she remembered the Marquis saying to Martha:

"If you want to go into a Convent, I will arrange with the Archbishop of Westminster Cathedral, that you go into the very best one there is."

A Convent!

It was the only refuge she could think of at the moment.

She was not a Catholic, but as she had told Father Anthony she wished to become one. Any Convent would therefore take her, and there would be no difficulties.

She took her hat from the wardrobe and picking up her gloves and her hand-bag she went down the stairs.

When she reached the hall Carter the Butler was there and she said:

"Please will you call me a Hackney Carriage?"

"A Hackney Carriage, Miss?" Carter exclaimed. "It'll take only a moment for me to send to the Mews for one of His Lordship's carriages."

"No, I want a Hackney Carriage!" Zia said firmly.

"But, you can't be going out alone, Miss?"

"I do not see why you should try to stop me," Zia answered, "and I do not think you have the right to do so."

Carter looked embarrassed.

He knew something was wrong, and after what had happened he could hardly believe Miss Langley would contemplate going driving alone again.

"Now, listen, Miss," he said in the kindly tones of an old family servant, "I knows His Lordship would not want you to go out alone in a public vehicle, when our horses and coachmen are available in the Mews."

"I have . . . to go . . . I have to!" Zia said desperately.

"I think, Miss, that first you should speak to Mr. Barrett."

Zia felt as if once again she was being confined against her will.

Because it was a warm and sunny day the front-door was open, and without saying another word she passed Carter, running down the steps and out through the short drive into Park Lane.

Carter stood staring after her in astonishment.

Then he said to one of the footmen who he thought was more sensible than the others:

"Follow Miss Langley, James, and don't let her out of your sight. If she takes a Hackney Carriage, get another one and follow her. Do you understand?"

"Yes, Mr. Carter!"

Carter put his hand into his pocket, took out the first coins he found in it, and gave them to the boy.

"Hurry now, hurry!" he said urgently. "And don't lose her, whatever you do!"

As James ran into Park Lane, Carter walked so quickly that he too was almost running to Mr. Barrett's office.

Zia found a Hackney Carriage that was for hire almost immediately and told the driver to take her to Westminster Cathedral.

As it was a warm day the hood was down, but to Zia there was no sunshine, only an impenetrable darkness.

She was driven very much more slowly than she would have been behind the Marquis's spirited and well-bred horses.

It was however not very far to Westminster Cathedral, and all the time she was fighting back her tears.

She was determined she would speak sensibly to the Cardinal so that he would understand her anxiety to go into a Convent immediately.

"I shall never . . . love anybody . . . else," she told herself miserably, "so how can I . . . stay in the . . . world when I might see . . . him with his . . . wife . . . and . . . his . . . children?"

She shut her eyes feeling the pain it gave her.

It was an agony to think that perhaps his love for her had been false and, as Lady Caton had said, he was merely trying to evade his responsibilities.

"How can I . . . live without . . . him?" she asked despairingly.

She wished that last night she had been able to throw herself into the Thames and be drowned, as Father Proteus had been.

When she reached Westminster Cathedral she paid off the Hackney Carriage and walked into the huge Basilica.

There was the scent of incense and hundreds of candles were flickering in the side Chapels.

She genuflected and stood for a moment looking at the High Altar, then seeing a man who looked like a Verger she went up to him and said:

"I wish to see His Eminence the Cardinal. Is that possible?"

Her appearance obviously impressed him for without hesitation the man replied:

"I'm not certain, Madam, if His Eminence is available, but Monseigneur St. Ives is I know in the Cathedral, and perhaps you would speak with him?"

"Thank you very much," Zia answered.

She was led down a side aisle and behind the Altar until the man who was leading her asked her to wait a moment outside a closed door.

She stood feeling more numb than anything else.

It was as if the agony she felt at first after she had listened to the Marquis's visitor had stunned her.

Now she felt almost detached from herself.

The door in front of her opened and the man who had escorted her there said:

"The Monseigneur will see you, Madam."

Zia walked forward and found she was in a small room, rather like an office.

There were religious books on a number of shelves and the Monseigneur, a kindly-looking elderly man, was sitting at a desk.

As she entered he rose and she curtsied to him as she had done when she was in the Convent to Father Anthony and later to Father Proteus.

"You wanted to see me?" the Monseigneur asked gently, holding out his hand.

"I . . . I have a . . . request to make, Monseigneur," Zia replied.

He indicated a chair on the other side of the desk and they both sat down.

"Now, what can I do for you?" the Priest enquired.

Zia drew in her breath.

"I want to . . . become a Catholic . . . and enter a Convent. I am . . . wealthy . . . so that I can . . . endow any Convent . . . which will . . . receive me."

"You have thought this over carefully?" the Monseigneur asked after a slight pause.

"Yes . . . and I have already had some . . . instruction at the Convent I attended in Cornwall."

"What is its name?"

"The Convent of the Holy Thorn," Zia replied. "It was partly a School . . . and Father Anthony who was . . . in charge is very ill . . . and it is . . . unlikely he will . . . recover."

"I have heard of this Convent," the Monseigneur said.

"I have been there for the last two years," Zia explained, "but then I was . . . persuaded to . . . try to live in the . . . Social World, but now . . . I know it is . . . not for me."

As she spoke she could not prevent the agony she was feeling sounding in her voice.

The Monseigneur bent forward to say:

"I think you are unhappy, my child. Is that the reason why you wish to enter a Convent?"

Because it was impossible for Zia to speak, she nodded her head and he said gently:

"Unhappiness is not always the best reason for dedicating your life to God. I would like you to think over the possibility of remaining in the Social World to which you belong for a little while longer before you make any hasty decision which will so greatly affect your whole life."

"I have . . . made my . . . decision," Zia answered. "Please take me . . . take me . . . now!"

She looked at the Monseigneur and her eyes filled with tears.

Then as he hesitated, obviously feeling for words, the door behind him was opened and the same Verger who had escorted Zia said:

"A gentleman to see you, Monseigneur!"

Zia did not look round, but she heard footsteps behind her and to her astonishment a deep voice said:

"Zia! How could you do anything so foolish?"

Zia still did not turn her head.

Instead she put her hands over her eyes and could not stop herself from crying.

The Marquis looked down at her, then he said:

"You must forgive me, Monseigneur. I am the Marquis of Okehampton. I saw my Ward driving alone in a Hackney Carriage past Buckingham Palace, and I followed her here, knowing there must be something wrong."

"I think there is," Monseigneur St. Ives answered, "and I suggest, My Lord, that I leave you alone together to discuss your differences. Afterwards, if you or the young lady wishes to see me I will be available."

"You are very kind," the Marquis said, "and I am extremely grateful."

Immediately the Monseigneur went from the room closing the door behind him and the Marquis sat down in a chair that was beside Zia's.

"Now, tell me what has happened?" he said gently. "What is wrong? I could hardly believe it possible when I saw you driving alone."

Zia did not reply, and after a moment he said: "Why did you come here?"

"I . . . I want to . . . enter a . . . Convent!" Zia murmured.

"And leave me?"

"Y-yes."

The monosyllable was hardly audible, but the Marquis heard it and after a moment he said:

"I thought you loved me!"

"I do . . . I do!" Zia sobbed. "But you belong to . . . her and . . . I cannot . . . stay in a world . . . where I might . . . see you with . . . somebody else as your . . . w-wife!"

The Marquis stiffened. Then he said:

"Stop crying, my darling, and tell me exactly what has happened, and why it has upset you."

Zia did not answer, nor did she take her hands from her eyes, but she was no longer crying.

Very gently the Marquis bent forward to pull her hands from her face.

Her cheeks were stained with tears, her long eyelashes were wet and when she looked at him he saw the pain and agony in her eyes.

It made him go down on one knee beside her and put his arms round her shoulders.

"What has happened, my darling, my precious little love?" he asked.

He could feel Zia trembling and she looked down.

Then in a voice he could hardly hear she said:

"The . . . Lady said . . . she was . . . carrying your . . . baby . . . and that you had promised to . . . marry her!"

The Marquis was very still. Then he said:

"Look at me, my precious, I want you to look at me."

Slowly she raised her eyes to his and when she had done so he said:

"We are in a Holy place, the House of God, and I swear to you by everything I hold sacred, on the memory of my mother whom I loved as you loved yours, that no woman, including the one who spoke to you, has ever had a child by me!"

Zia stared at him.

"You have to believe me," the Marquis said, "because I think your instinct and your love for me would tell you if I was lying, just as it will also make you know that I am telling the truth."

He saw a little flicker of light in Zia's eyes before she said:

"Then . . . why . . . why should . . . she say such a . . . thing?"

"Because she had made up her mind to marry me, even while her husband was still living."

"But . . . you do not . . . want to . . . m-marry her?"

"I have never wanted to marry any woman, except you!" the Marquis said truthfully.

"Th-then I do not . . . understand . . . why . . .?"

"Listen to me, my precious," the Marquis said. "I will not pretend to you that there has not been a number of women in my life. I am a man, and if a beautiful woman wishes to honour me by giving herself to me, I would be inhuman if I did not accept such favours."

He saw that Zia was listening and he went on:

"But you are intelligent enough to understand that a man may desire a woman because she is beautiful, and that what he feels for her is an appreciation such as he would feel for a beautiful flower, or the joy which is expressed in music, or the warmth of the sun."

He felt Zia relax a little as he went on:

"But while it can be a delightful sensation, it is not real love – the love I have for you, my dearest Heart, and which I believe you have for me. What we have found together is the love that comes from God, the love a man has for the one special woman in his life, who is actually the other half of himself."

He drew Zia a little closer to him as he said:

"It is the very special love that your father had for your mother, and my father had for mine. It is the love that is Divine, and which could never be spoilt by lies, deception, or treachery."

Zia made a little murmur and the Marquis said:

"Just as Father Proteus was a bad man, so the woman you have just met is bad beneath the beauty of her face. We simply have to forget them both!"

"But . . . suppose," Zia said in a very small voice, "she . . . tries to . . . hurt you?"

"That she has done already, by upsetting you!" the Marquis said. "I had no idea, when her husband has not yet been buried, that she would come to my house, or that you would see her and she would tell you a lie."

There was silence. Then Zia said:

"I am . . . sorry . . . forgive me . . . I should have . . . trusted . . . you."

"That is what I want you to do," the Marquis said, "and you must forgive me . . . that I have sinned in the past, which I can swear to you here in the Cathedral, is something I shall never do in the future."

Zia gave a little sob.

"I love you . . . I love . . . you!" she whispered, "but . . . when I . . . came here . . . I . . . I wanted to . . . d-die!"

"And now we both want to live!" the Marquis said. "And I want you to come home, for you have to choose your wedding-gown in which you will become my wife tomorrow."

As he spoke he drew Zia to her feet.

"I love you with all my heart and all my soul!" he said. "That, my darling, is something I have never said to any other woman, for it would not have been true!"

"And . . . I love . . . you!" Zia whispered. "You fill the . . . whole world . . . the sky and the sea . . . and I know if I . . . lost you I would have . . . nothing . . . nothing at all!"

"You will never lose me," the Marquis vowed.

She thought he would kiss her.

But, as if he was thinking of the Holy place in which they were standing, he raised her hands to his lips and kissed first one, then the other.

Then he drew her towards the door.

When they reached it they saw on duty outside the Verger who had brought the Marquis to Monseigneur St. Ives's Study.

"May I speak to the Monseigneur?" the Marquis enquired.

"I regret, Sir, the Monseigneur is at present in the Confessional," the man replied, "but he asked me to tell you that he would pray for you."

"Will you thank the Monseigneur," the Marquis said, "and say that I will be sending him a thank-offering."

The Marquis walked on down the aisle with Zia, and as they did so she felt as if the Saints in the Chapels they passed were giving them a special blessing.

Then they were outside in the sunshine and she saw the Marquis's Phaeton drawn by two horses which were being held by a groom.

They drove back the way Zia had come past Buckingham Palace.

They did not speak, but Zia felt as though the sun had never been more bright and it seemed to envelop them with an aura of happiness.

When they arrived back at Oke House Zia was aware there was an expression of relief on Carter's face as he saw that she was with the Marquis.

As she ran up to her bedroom to take off her hat, Carter informed the Marquis in a low voice what had occurred and how anxious he had been.

"By sheer chance, I saw Miss Langley driving past Buckingham Palace, where I had been to see His Royal Highness who was holding an Investiture," the Marquis explained. "However, it was sensible and very intelligent of you, Carter, to have sent somebody after her. But then I know I can always rely on you."

The Butler was beaming. Then the Marquis asked:

"Is Lady Caton still here?"

"She left a quarter-of-an-hour ago, M'Lord," he replied, "having waited for nearly an hour."

"If she calls again," the Marquis said firmly, "I am not at home!"

"I had no idea Miss Langley was in the Study, M'Lord!"

"I realise that, but do not make another mistake before we leave tomorrow morning for the Castle, and say nothing of this to Her Ladyship."

"No, of course not, M'Lord. It would only upset her."

The Marquis wanted to say it had upset him, but by the mercy of God everything was now all right.

Then as if he could not wait another minute to see Zia he said:

"We will have tea in the Drawing-Room."

He went upstairs to wait for Zia to come from her bedroom.

*

There was so much that Zia wanted to see in the Castle when they arrived after stopping on the way for luncheon, but the Marquis said firmly that she was to rest.

They were to be married at five o'clock and he sent her to her bedroom until then.

She guessed one of his reasons was that he wished to see that the Chapel was filled with flowers, and later she found she had not been mistaken.

It was a small but very beautiful Chapel which had been built at the same time as the Castle and to which few alterations had been made over the years.

Only the Marquis, she thought, could have contrived that it was filled with Arum lilies, and their fragrance scented the air.

It was the perfect background for her white gown.

It had arrived just before they left London, and had been ordered by the Marquis almost from the moment he had asked her to be his wife.

"How could you have been so wonderful in planning everything so cleverly?" she asked him as they drove through the beautiful countryside towards the Castle.

"I want everything in your life to be perfect," he said, "as perfect, my precious, as our love."

"That is so . . . perfect that there are no . . . words to . . . describe it," Zia said softly.

It was what the Marquis thought too. Harry, who was to be his Best Man, had said to him last night after dinner:

"You are marrying exactly the right person in taking Zia as your wife!"

"I love her!" the Marquis said fiercely.

He was afraid Harry was still thinking he was marrying her to be rid of Yasmin.

"I know that," Harry said. "I have never seen you looking so happy or so pleased with yourself!"

The Marquis laughed.

He knew it was true, he was happy.

He also was pleased to think he had been clever enough to find the one person in the world who he was sure was different from anybody else.

He had taken Zia to the Castle alone, and Harry had arranged to stay with friends who lived about two miles away.

"You realise," he said, "that everyone will want to tear my eyes out if I am the only guest at your marriage? They will all be expecting a 'slap-up' feast, with the Prince of Wales present, and at least half-a-dozen bridesmaids!"

"Then they will be disappointed!" the Marquis said. "This is exactly the sort of wedding I always wanted, but thought I would never be lucky enough to have."

"What you are really saying is that it is the sort of wedding that Zia wants too," Harry remarked.

"Of course!" the Marquis agreed. "After all she has been through, I am not having her upset by women being spiteful or men making eyes at her!"

Harry laughed.

"She is so beautiful that you will be kept busy fending off men like Charlie who will find her irresistible."

"I know that," the Marquis agreed, "but we are going to spend most of our time in the country, and men like Charlie will not be amongst our guests!"

The Marquis paused. Then he said:

"As a matter of fact, I do not intend to have any guests for a long time. I want Zia all to myself."

The way he spoke made Harry look at him enviously.

It was the sort of marriage he wanted himself if he ever found a woman he wished to marry.

But that could be said of every man who, like Charlie, flitted from *Boudoir* to *Boudoir*, inevitably to be bored and disappointed.

As the Marquis and Zia knelt side by side for the final blessing from the Chaplain they were holding hands.

It seemed to both of them that the vibrations which they felt emanating from within themselves was like a Divine Light.

They left the Chapel and without speaking to anybody, as the Marquis had arranged, they went up to Zia's bedroom, which had been his mother's.

The Marquis shut the door, then to Zia's surprise he did not take her in his arms, but drew her to the window.

They stood looking out at the garden, the lake which lay beyond it, and the great trees in the Park.

Beyond that there was a vista over the woods which eventually led to the sea.

For a moment the Marquis did not speak. Then he said:

"This is my world, my precious, which is now yours. I think we will both love it, rule over it, and try to give everybody who lives in it the same happiness that we have ourselves."

Zia gave a little exclamation and moved closer to him.

"Only . . . you could . . . think like . . . that," she said.

"It is the way you have taught me to think," he answered, "but it has been there in my heart, although I have never been able to express it until now."

He put his arms round her and there was no longer any need for words.

A long time later, when the sun was sinking and the rooks were going to roost in the trees, the Marquis said:

"I am wondering, my precious one, why you are so different from any woman I have ever known before."

"Am I . . . so different?" Zia asked. "You are so . . . wonderful . . . so utterly and completely . . . marvellous that when you made love to me I was . . . just a little afraid . . . as it was . . . so new to me . . . that you would not . . . feel the same . . . as I did."

"I felt all you felt, and more," the Marquis said, "and once again I am being truthful when I tell you that never has anything been so perfect or so glorious as loving you."

Zia gave a little cry.

"That is exactly what I wanted you to say . . . and please . . . darling . . . never grow . . . bored with . . . loving me."

"How could I be bored with anything that seems to carry me up to the Heaven in which you believe, and which makes me feel as if I hold an angel in my arms."

He bent over Zia and moved the softness of her hair back from her oval forehead.

"You are beautiful," he said, "but so are other women. What is it about you that is so different?"

"Tell me . . . please tell me what it is!"

"I know the answer," the Marquis said. "It is because you are good, and I have known few really good women in my life!"

"I am sure . . . that is not . . . true," Zia said, "but I want you to think I am."

"You are good, as my mother was," the Marquis said. "Until now I have never found anyone who could ever mean what she meant to me, but now there is you, and in many ways, you are very like her."

"I am . . . thrilled that you . . . should think . . . so," Zia murmured.

"I know, my beautiful little wife, that you are good in your heart and in your soul, and that is what I want you to be, and nothing shall spoil you."

The Marquis paused before he said in a different tone:

"If any man attempted to do so, I swear I would kill him!"

His voice seemed to ring out, then he was kissing Zia fiercely, demandingly, possessively.

His lips almost hurt her, and yet she was not afraid.

She knew this feeling of possessiveness was very much part of their love, and in fact love was not the soft, gentle sentimental thing she had thought it to be.

It was strong, vibrant, often violent, often disruptive, at the same time invincible and irresistible.

She knew it was love which had made the Marquis strong and clever enough to fight for her and to save her from Proteus.

It was love which in the future would enable them to battle against any obstacles or difficulties, for of course there would be some in their lives.

But he would always be the victor, always the conqueror, simply because his love gave him the strength to overcome evil and anything that was wrong or wicked.

The Marquis's kisses became more demanding, and she knew there was a fire in his eyes.

There was also a fire within him which made her know that while he worshipped her, he also desired her as a woman.

She could feel the same fire within herself and now it was flickering with the flames.

"I want you! My darling, I want you!" the Marquis said.

"I am . . . yours!" Zia murmured.

"Give me yourself, love me, for only God knows how much I love you!"

"I . . . love you . . . I love . . . you!"

The words seemed to burn with an intensity within them both.

Then as the Marquis made Zia his, they were swept together into the burning heart of the sun.

The glory of it enveloped them both with the Divine Light which comes from God which is Life itself and is eternal.